# MISTER MOM

**PIPER RAYNE**

## Mister Mom

Secrets and lies are a killer way to start any partnership—especially a horizontal one.

Now, I'm a glass half full kinda of guy, so, after the 'you're fired' speech was directed at me, I figure now's the time to be the screenwriter I came to sunny California to be. Unfortunately, there are about as many people trying to sell a script in L.A. as there are vegans in the pacific northwest.

But lucky for me, a few weeks ago my agent found an investor for my script. Hooray, all my problems are solved! NOT.

Because the investor will only agree to fund my film if I use one specific actress. And that one specific actress? Well of course, it just has to be the same actress I screwed over only months before. But she doesn't need to know about that one tiny detail, does she? All that matters is getting her to agree to do the film and I'll do whatever it takes. We can leave the past, in the past, right?

I thought my charm would win her over. Never would I have been prepared for the terms she laid out on the table.

**She needed a nanny.**
**I needed a lead actress.**
**Somehow I became The Manny.**

# MISTER Mom

## Dedication

*To all the step parents making a difference.*

## Vance

The wheels of the jet land on LAX's runway and anxiety causes my heart to pulsate in an unsteady rhythm. Escaping to my hometown was a nice vacation from reality, but now that I've returned to the City of Angels, who I used to be in this town is at the forefront of my mind.

Heading back to Climax Cove was a spur-of-the-moment decision. And by that, I mean I packed a bag within five minutes and hightailed it to the airport, paying way too fucking much money for a one-way ticket. Money an unemployed thirty-something guy shouldn't spend, even if I was rolling in it up until I was fired. I was very successful by anyone's standards, yes—but it's not like I was an A-list actor pulling in eight figures a year.

I pull my phone out, strapping my only piece of luggage, my backpack, to my back, and dial up my buddy Jagger on the way to arrivals.

No answer.

Typical.

Crossing my fingers that he didn't just land some hot

piece of ass and forget to pick me up at the airport, I head through baggage claim and out the automatic doors, taking a brief glance up at the dark sky with an absence of stars.

The tall oak trees have been replaced by palm trees, the tranquil scene of the evergreen mountains in the distance has vanished, leaving me with smog-filled air and a shit-ton of bustling people surrounding me.

My footsteps stop when I spot Jagger sitting on his expensive Harley Davidson motorcycle talking to a female police officer who's probably supposed to be directing traffic, but instead is giggling at something he's said.

He touches her shoulder and her hand leaves her holster to cover her laugh. I guess it only takes one flirtatious comment from Jagger Kale and someone has an opportunity to strip her of her weapon.

I make my approach and her hand moves to her gun as she eyes me from the corner of her vision. So, I underestimated her. Her attention causes Jagger to turn his head in my direction, his usual smirk splashed across his lips.

"Hey, man." He pops the kickstand out on the bike and hops off, circling around toward me and sticking his hand out for me to shake.

The police officer still has her eyes on me and I get that I might look a little less put together from my time in Climax Cove, but I still look like I belong in L.A.

I shake Jagger's hand at the same time as I shake my head.

His smirk deepens, continuing our non-verbal conversation. Me saying he's an idiot for flirting with a cop and him saying, *Look at her tits, how can I not?*

Our hands part and I stand there like a third wheel as she texts him her phone number.

"Make sure you use it," she says in what I guess is her best cop voice. It's so authoritative that my gaze and my mind flickers to her handcuffs, wondering how well she uses them.

Jagger winks at her, most likely thinking the same as me. "Don't worry, sweetheart, I never forget to call."

The cop looks at me and I lower my raised eyebrows. Jagger's not a total manwhore, he just enjoys the single life to the fullest. At least he stays away from his clients... his very *elite* list of clients. He's a top talent agent in the industry and his list is filled with top-grade tits and ass, but in all the time I've known him he's never crossed the line with any of them.

I admire the cop's physique as her ass sways with her belt around her midsection while she walks back into the middle of the roadway to direct the non-stop rotation of cars.

"Seriously?"

"What?" Jagger holds his hands up, a small smirk on his face. Yeah, he knows exactly what I'm questioning.

"Let's ignore the fact that your flirting caused the cars be parked four deep and she didn't seem to care as long as she was in the running to suck you off."

He chuckles, glancing over his shoulder at the line-up of cars parked, waiting for their loved ones.

"And we'll ignore that you're parked in the limo and cab lane."

He looks around innocently like the plethora of posted signs aren't visible.

"What I can't ignore is the fact I'm standing here looking at your *motorcycle*."

His chuckle morphs into a full-out laugh. "Hey, I brought you a helmet." He pulls one out of his side satchel. The hot pink one he makes girls wear when he takes them for a ride along the coast—Jagger's form of foreplay, from what I can tell.

"Jagger." I sigh. "Seriously, man, where's the Aston Martin?"

He straddles his bike, positioning his helmet over his head, and kicks the stand, ready to ride. "It's at my place in

Malibu. I've spent the last few nights at my condo in the city. No chance I was driving all the way back to get my car."

I shake my head in annoyance and stand there in disbelief that he wants my dick pressed to his ass while we inchworm our way through L.A. traffic.

"Stop the drama and hop on. You not secure enough in your manhood to ride bitch?" He hands over the helmet and I bite back a curse while I straddle the bike and click on the helmet, all while trying to keep my dick as far away from him as possible.

The motorcycle roars to life and I grab the sissy bar behind me, using all my strength to prevent my ass from sliding forward toward him.

Jagger does what Jagger does best, going no holds barred as we head through the Sepulveda Boulevard Tunnel.

———

WHAT FEELS like hours but really is only forty-five minutes later, I jump off his bike, thankful to be able to put some space between me and my friend.

"Thanks," I mumble, climbing the stairs to my second-floor condo.

"Whoa, hold up."

The loud pipes silence and the stand of his bike echoes in the dark night.

"I'm tired and I want to get some sleep." I make the excuse before giving him a chance to say anything.

I reach the first landing, now only a few doors away from escape, but Jagger's footsteps are quickening on the cement behind me.

"What? I give you a ride home and you don't even ask me in for a drink?" he asks and laughs.

"I don't even know what I have."

"No worries, I'll run down to Leo's if need be."

Leo's our friend, who lives on the first floor of my building.

"I'm not in the mood." I try the excuse again.

"Oh, come on. We need to talk about how you ran back home to Mommy."

I stop at the top of the stairs and narrow my eyes. "Yeah, that's not going to happen. Might as well call the cop from earlier."

He chuckles, walking backwards past me toward condo number two hundred and seven.

"Don't do it," I warn.

He raises his knuckles to the door.

"Jagger, seriously, give me a day and then we can talk."

He motions to knock and I shake my head, walking over to my own condo door. "I'll just lock you out."

There's no point in rushing. Leo, the owner of condo two hundred and seven, has a key. A key he's been using the past six weeks to water my one plant and check up on things.

The loud knock of Jagger's fist on the door bounces down the open hallway as I insert my own key into the lock of my condo. And then it's the sound of Cooper, Leo's dog, barking and running toward the door. I can already picture his paws skidding to a stop, waiting for Leo to catch up, his tail wagging with impatience as he waits for his owner to open the door for their guest.

"Jesus," Jagger says.

I laugh, knowing exactly what just happened. Cooper jumped up and licked his face.

"Can't you put him through obedience training or something?" Jagger asks.

I shake my head and open my door.

"He's been twice. He just loves you, man." Leo's voice sounds out.

And then a door shuts and two sets of footsteps walk closer to the stairs along with four galloping ones that snake their way into my condo without an invitation.

I'm knocked down on the couch, Cooper on my back and his tongue on my neck.

"Relax, Coop," I say, planting my hand on my neck to push him away.

"Cooper!" Leo's authoritative voice rings out and Cooper listens, moving off my back, but sitting down next to me, drool falling from his panting tongue onto my floor.

Jagger moves to the kitchen, opening the fridge and shutting it quickly, plugging his nose. "Fuck, that's rancid."

"I probably should've cleaned that out for you." Leo shrugs, patting Cooper on the head as he sits next to him by the chair.

"That's all right. Listen, guys, great to see you, but I gotta crash."

Jagger sits in the chair opposite me, showing no signs of leaving.

I purposely stand, because staying seated would be an invitation to stay, which they're not. Invited, I mean.

"That's the polite way of saying 'get the fuck out,'" I continue when neither of them lifts their ass from my furniture.

Jagger's gaze shifts to the couch and back to me and back to the couch.

"One question," I warn and sit down, propping my feet on the coffee table in front of me.

"What are you going to do now?" Leo asks.

I give the guy props—he hasn't asked me once where I went or why.

"I'm going to make my script into a movie."

Jagger winces, shaking his head. Both have read my script. They know the years I took perfecting it and how much I've wanted to put it out there, but how scared I've been.

"Are you sure? I mean after..." Jagger trails off.

"I'm sure. I went back home and the one thing I realized is fear is for cowards. I'm not a coward. I wasn't one when I left Climax Cove to start a new life here and I'm not one now."

The sad part was I had to learn that I needed to grow a set from my sister. She's always been so ballsy and take-charge, go after what you want. It was easy to forget being so far away from her all this time.

"Good for you." Leo, the cheerleader of our group, nods with encouragement.

"It's going to be hard, but if you want my help, I'm here." Jagger slides his ass up on the chair, resting his elbows on his knees. "You thinking of selling it to a studio or going the independent route?"

"Independent. We know I have the chops to the produce the thing and I want the freedom that'll bring. A studio will just fuck it up to make it more commercial," I say.

Jagger nods and I can tell he's in business mode. His jaw is set and the deep-set line between his brows is on fully display. "We need to find an investor first."

"I'd love your help."

Leo and I stare at him. He pulls out his phone, already scrolling through his contacts. "My dad mentioned someone looking to take on a new project a month or so back. Give me a few weeks and let me see if I can put something together."

He stands and steps over Leo's legs and Cooper, who's now sprawled out on my living room floor. "Get some rest," he says over his shoulder. Jagger's phone is already planted to his ear before he leaves the condo. "Hey, Dad. Remember that investor you mentioned..." His conversation trails into silence as the door shuts behind him.

"Let's go, Coop." Leo nudges his dog with his foot and Cooper slowly wobbles onto his legs and prances toward the door. "We'll catch up tomorrow." He raises his hand in the air and disappears behind the door, too.

If I'd known it was that easy to get my two buddies out of my condo, I would've tried that ages ago.

**2**

**Vance**

I grab my vibrating phone off the nightstand and roll over, bringing it to my ear. "Yeah?" My voice is groggy and raw from the early-morning wake-up call.

"You know jet lag isn't a thing when you've only been to Oregon, don't you?"

Jagger.

"Who do I have to pay not to hear your voice for twenty-four hours?" I sit up in my bed, the sheet falling to my waist.

"You've been home for weeks. Besides, I wouldn't be so pissy. I've got great news."

"What time is it?" I scrunch my eyes and rub a hand over them before glancing over to the clock on the cable box.

*Does it really say eleven? Where the hell did the morning go?*

"Let's just say, McDonald's breakfast is over."

Like health nut Jagger has ever eaten a Big Mac.

"What's this news you speak of?"

"I found someone interested in investing."

I bolt up, swinging my legs over the side of my bed. "Yeah?"

Jagger's reputation is for putting deals together that seem

impossible at the outset, and he's always been one to work fast, but this has to be a record, even for him.

"Finally up, huh? Say, 'Thank you, Jagger, for working your magic.'" He chuckles and I hear his assistant paging him over the intercom in his office. "Give me two, Vic."

"Give me some details. Who is it?"

"Not until you say, 'Thank you, Jagger.'" He chuckles with amusement I'm used to by now. The man takes nothing too seriously. Actually, strike that. He's only serious about two things—money and his career.

"Thank you, Jagger. Now can I have the details?"

"Sure thing," his assistant, Victoria, says in the background through his office phone. "But he's threatening to hang up if you don't have time for him."

"I'm talking to Vance. Hold up."

"Tell Vance hello," Victoria says.

"I say hello in return." I have no idea how this turned into a game of telephone.

"You can tell her yourself when you pick me up for lunch this afternoon." Jagger pauses.

"Lunch?"

"Yeah, get all prettied up because you owe me big time for this one. See you at one."

The line goes dead and I place my phone on the bed, running my hands down my face.

If I wasn't positive he did indeed work his usual magic in the two weeks since I gave him the go-ahead on my script, I'd stand him up, but the man has me by my balls and he knows it.

———

AT ONE O'CLOCK THAT AFTERNOON, I drag my ass into Jagger's office.

"Hey, Victoria." I wave, bypassing her sparse desk. "Props on not getting too comfortable."

She rolls her eyes and nods. As soon as Jagger finds another assistant she'll go back to her usual job of running the office. Victoria is the only person Jagger trusts to fill in when he's between assistants—which is often—but she refuses to work for him directly, knowing how demanding he can be. I can only assume he keeps her around because she's good at what she does.

"Afternoon, Vance. Go on in. He's probably just in there jerking off."

I stop at the edge of her desk and cock an eyebrow, then laugh. "You should really think of staying put in that chair. I think he may have just met his match with you."

She turns in her chair and stands, grabbing a stack of papers. "Not sure I'm ready to admit my fate just yet." She touches my shoulder in a friendly way as she passes me by walking down the hall.

I push open the doors to Jagger's office, thankful that Victoria's assumption that his dick would be in his fisted hand isn't true. He waves me in with one hand, his feet propped up on his desk as he leans back in his chair.

Grabbing a water from his cooler by the couch, I take a seat, twisting open the bottle. He continues to work a deal on the phone for some actress while I read through the latest edition of *Hollywood Reporter* that he has on the table.

Once he hangs up, he rounds his desk and sits in the chair across from me. "Actresses are so temperamental," he laments.

"Tell me about it," I say, still thumbing through the magazine. "One bonus of being unemployed."

The corner of Jagger's mouth tips down and he rests his ankle on his knee. "You might not be unemployed for long."

I toss the magazine on the table and grab my bottle of water. "You got me down here. Let's hear what you've got."

The entire ride here I've tried to keep my expectations low. I'm not a nobody in this town, but since I'll be releasing my script under my real name, Vance Rose, and not under the name I used when I was a producer, there's a chance Jagger couldn't get my script into the right hands.

"I know you didn't want people to know that you're Ryder Stone, that you were the executive producer of a TV show that won six Emmys its first year..."

My face shows no emotion. I've dealt firsthand with political bullshit in this industry. No one is immune to it. Somehow getting fired took the gleam off the coveted awards that used to line the bookshelf in my condo. They're currently shoved in a cardboard box at the bottom of my closet.

"But?"

All he does is nod. Slowly. No words.

"Continue."

"I had to use your background to get your foot in the door. Besides, they promised to keep it under wraps."

"Heard that before," I sneer, downing another gulp of my water.

"Are you going to listen to me or sit there pissed off and wallowing? I mean, getting a script made into a movie is as difficult as finding the next wholesome actress from the Midwest with raw talent."

"You seem to find them just fine," I deadpan.

Jagger's not at all into my humor and I should probably drop the attitude, but the bitterness of being fired for such a bullshit reason still eats away at my insides.

"Because I'm Jagger fucking Kale." He stands. "Get your ass up. I'm not telling you shit until you eat something. You're always an asshole on an empty stomach." Snatching his phone from his desk, he tucks it into his suit jacket and holds his office door open for me.

"Just tell me."

"Fuck you. Let's go."

I pass by him to find Victoria's gaze on us.

"I'll be back in a few hours. Call me with anything important." He doesn't wait for her to answer and beelines it toward the elevators.

"See you, Victoria. Keep rocking the pant suits." I wink and a smile tips the edges of her lips.

"I know better than to show any of the goods around here." She winks back and then focuses her attention to her computer. "Keep him out as long as you can, please."

"Let's go, drama queen." Jagger's hand is on the doors of the elevator.

"I'll do my best," I say as I backstep to the elevator.

The doors shut, cutting off my view of Victoria silently laughing to herself while shaking her head.

"Don't flirt with my assistant. If I can't touch her, neither can you." He presses the lobby button with his knuckle.

"Why can't I touch her?"

"Please. The last thing I fucking need is her asking me shit like, 'Did he say anything about me?' 'Do you know why he's not texting me back?' 'Why doesn't he want to see me anymore?'" he says in his best impression of a woman's voice. Which is pretty bad, for the record. "Besides. We're friends. That means you don't take what's mine."

I scoff. "She's not yours."

"She might be if she ever decides to quit." He raises a brow.

I stifle a laugh. "What's to say she'll quit?"

"They all quit."

The elevator dings and the doors open. We push our way through the crowd waiting to file in, eventually reaching the rotating doors and making our way outside. The sun heats my face and our steps echo on the concrete as we head to the parking garage.

"I think she's a keeper, man. She's put up with your shit for this long." I place my hand on his shoulder.

He side-glances me. "None of them are keepers because I'm too enticing. They know I won't lay a hand on them until they don't work for me."

"You should really hire dudes."

"Yeah, no, thanks." He spots his Ferrari and pulls out his keys, unlocking the car and turning off the alarm. Did you think as arrogant as Jagger is, he wouldn't have a car like a Ferrari? He's got a whole arsenal of expensive cars.

We climb into his car and he roars out of the garage, easing off the brakes before he hits the street.

Traveling at Mach speed the entire way, we arrive at an ocean-side restaurant a little off the tourists' radar.

"Should've known you'd want to discuss my future over fish tacos." I shake my head as we head into the shack Jagger likes to claim he made famous.

"Who doesn't love fish tacos?" He tucks his keys into his suit pants and makes a display of putting his phone on vibrate before he pushes it down into the inside pocket of his jacket.

"Holy shit, do I really get Jagger Kale all to myself?"

He rolls his eyes and waves to the waitress, who he's screwed—out on the deck after closing time. But that's his story. If only I could get the visual out of my head every time we come here.

She points to a free table by the open window and we head there and take a seat.

"Okay, you've got me here. Tell me what the hell is going on." I rest my forearms on the table, taking a deep breath, waiting to hear if what he has to say makes me want to drown myself in the ocean.

He chuckles. "Well, I got a deal for you and it's good. The investor is from the East Coast and likes the feel of the story. Says it reminds her of her own summer love story. She only has one stipulation. Even so, if you ask me, you should be kissing my Italian loafers right about now."

I stare at him, waiting for him to get on with it, when the waitress saunters over and rests her hip on the table, facing Jagger with crossed arms.

"You didn't call," she says, irritation ringing out in her tone.

He leans forward and brushes her long red hair back, exposing her bare, freckled shoulder. The stiffness of her posture falters a bit.

"Maybe you gave me the wrong phone number," he says, all innocence.

She shakes her head. "I didn't."

"Well, I don't know, honey, I called."

He didn't.

She pulls her order pad from her pocket, scribbles her digits down on a piece of paper and slides it across the table. "This is the right one. Use it. Two Heinekens?" She shoots me a fleeting glance.

Oh, good, she realizes I'm here.

Jagger tucks the piece of paper into the front pocket of his shirt and pats his chest. "Safckccping." He winks and I let out an exasperated sigh, earning both their glares.

She leaves and Jagger's gaze follows her to the bar. "I'm an ass man. What about you?"

"Jagger," I say, but his attention is still focused on the waitress.

He turns back to me and smiles that 'okay, okay, give me a break' smile. "The investor wants the leading lady to be Layla Andrews."

I swear everything around me disappears and I look upon

my friend with tunnel vision. It took me until right now to realize why he's stranded me at the fish taco place outside of the city—I can't go anywhere. He's my ride back, although if I could surf, I might just paddle out into the ocean.

"She won't do it."

The waitress, whose name is Heidi based on the name tag pinned on her stretched t-shirt, drops the Heinekens on the table and I down half of mine before placing it back on the table. I draw in a deep breath and stare out to the abyss of the ocean.

"She will," Jagger says with more confidence than he should given the situation.

I look back and Heidi is gone and to my surprise Jagger isn't wearing a smug look on his face. Instead he's serious.

"Fuck, Jagger. Why on earth would she do me a favor? I fucked her over on that job, or have you forgotten?"

He leans forward, his hands clasped over his beer. "She only knows Ryder Stone and she has no idea what you look like."

He points out the one good thing about being behind the scenes in this industry. If I fuck you over, there's a good chance you wouldn't know me if you just walked past me in a coffee shop.

"So you want me to lie to her?"

He shrugs. "Just don't volunteer the information. It's more like... creative information engineering. Your script is written under your real name. Plus, once it's a million-dollar box office success she won't care that you screwed her out of that other role."

I bring my beer to my lips, contemplating his words.

"Not to mention, she's on some big set working right now. She probably doesn't even care anymore."

"What set?" I ask. She should have had a recurring role on *Abandoned*, the TV show I was fired from, but I convinced the casting director that she was just a glorified child actress and that audiences would never buy her in the serious role the script dictated.

"She's with Chris Pratt on that new movie of his."

"Fuck!" I down the rest of my beer.

"It's not opposite him. It's a small role. There's a good chance she'll end up on the cutting-room floor." Jagger takes a sip of his own beer. "I tried to get a hold of her this morning, but her agent's assistant, told me she's filming this entire week. Her agent is at the Sundance Film Festival and isn't returning my calls. I spoke with Layla briefly. You need to go to set to pitch the idea to her."

"Can't it wait until after she's done filming or her agent gets back?"

Heidi comes over and places two plates of fish tacos in front of us. Yeah, we're probably here too much. She eyes Jagger, licks her lips and then lets her finger run up his arm as she walks away.

"No. The investor wants it done this week. She wants to film scenes in Chicago while the weather is nice. Which means we're on the clock to have a crew out there this summer."

"Who is this investor, by the way?"

"All you need to know is that her name is Hannah and she has money."

I blow out a stream of air, resting my fork on my plate. "This is all going so fast."

Jagger laughs. "Isn't this what you wanted? If all goes well, you'll be a celebrity script writer inside of two years." He chomps down on his taco, his tie tossed over his shoulder, his jacket resting on the chair next to him. Totally out of place among the beach bums and surfers who really made this place famous.

"I don't much care for the deception factor."

Jagger swallows his mouthful. "Grow up, Vance. This is Hollywood. The whole industry was built on selling lies to the public. You want your movie or not?"

I nod, biting the inside of my cheek. My sister Charlie would kick my ass for what I'm about to do. But in all truthfulness, maybe it all worked out for the better. I mean, Layla's in a film with Chris Pratt. She might not have gotten that gig if she'd gotten the role in *Abandoned*. She should be thanking me. Plus, if my movie is a success, that totally trumps a small role in a television series. Right? Definitely.

"All right. Tell me where to find her."

He smiles over another mouthful of taco. "That's my boy." He winks.

## 3

### Vance

I lower my ball cap to shield my face. You'd think I was Harry Styles from the way I've been peering around corners and hiding behind set pieces to try to escape recognition while walking through the studio lot. I should've sent Jagger to present the damn script to her. I won't even get into the prima donna treatment Layla Andrews expects. Seriously, why the fuck am I here delivering this script? I suppose a courier service is too good for her.

*Fucking actresses.*

In some ways knowing she's as self-involved as all this makes me not feel as bad about screwing her over in the past. Everyone stamped my forehead with 'jackass,' but look at what she has me doing now. Jumping through fucking hoops. If I didn't need the investor so bad, I'd say, *Fuck you, I'll cast my lead actress myself.* Sadly, that's not the case. I need the money this investment lady is offering.

Layla Andrews' name is stuck on the outside of her trailer, so I knock, eager to escape inside.

The door flies open and a woman in her fifties shakes her

head, her shoulder knocking mine as she bounds down the stairs like there's a billow of smoke about to follow her.

"Hey," I greet her but she never stops.

"You can tell Miss Andrews I'm done," she yells over her shoulder.

A granola bar flies out of the door and hits her in the back. When I turn back to the trailer the culprit is a blond-haired boy who's squinting at her, hands on his hips. He looks like he's trying to do some kind of voodoo crap on her.

The woman picks up the granola bar, cocks her hand back, but I grip her wrist before she can whip it back at the boy.

*What the hell is she thinking?*

Her hand opens and the granola bar drops to the ground. "He's your problem now."

I look behind me to see who she's talking to but, nope, there's still just me.

I turn back, but the woman is stalking away, her feet hitting the pavement so hard you'd expect there to be potholes in her wake.

My head slowly rotates back to the little boy, who's standing there, staring back at me.

"Who are you?" he asks, his hands still resting on his hips.

"Vance."

He stands there, his fiery eyes not dimming in the slightest.

"And your name is?" I ask.

"My mom told me not to talk to strangers." The trailer door slams shut.

Great. I walk up the few steps and knock on the door again.

Silence greets me.

I knock again.

More silence.

My hand moves to the handle and it turns in my palm.

I inch the door open and peek in, but the little bastard kicks it shut, slamming me in the head with it. Now I know what that bald guy felt like in *Home Alone*.

"Shit." I squeeze my eyes shut in pain. My back falls to the door and I slide down until my ass is on the step and my hands are covering both sides of my head.

"Go away. I have a big monster in here and he's going to eat you alive." The kid's muffled voice sounds from the other side of the door.

"No worries. Nothing is worth this." I stand and walk down the last couple stairs until I remember how young the kid is. I'm not great with ages, but he seems younger than my buddy Dane's son for sure, and he's only eight.

So, against my better judgement, I trudge back up the stairs, squinting into the glare of the sun reflecting off the trailer.

I knock again.

"ROOOAAAARRRR!" I hear on the other side, followed by a bunch of scraping sounds.

My lips tip up into a smile. The kid actually thinks I'm buying the monster story.

I knock again.

Fists pound on the door in a rhythmic manner.

This kid could have a career as a sound engineer in his future.

"Hey, kid, I'm just looking for your mom."

"She's in the shower." He doesn't miss a beat, but the monster illusion has vanished.

Not to mention there's no showers in the trailers. This is a smaller one. I'm sure Chris Pratt has one in his trailer, but Layla apparently hasn't earned that privilege yet.

"Okay, I'll just wait then."

More silence. I'm not trying to freak the kid out, but

right now the only thing standing between him and a six o'clock news story on the abduction of an up-and-coming Hollywood starlet's son is me.

"She's going to be a long time," he says.

"I have nowhere else to be." I sit down on the step and within a minute the sunshine starts to warm me, seeping into my skin. Thank God, it's winter and not summer. Otherwise, I'd be sweating my balls off.

"You should go." For the first time, I hear shakiness in his voice.

Shit, he's scared.

I turn toward the door and I know he can't see me, but I plaster on my biggest smile, hoping that shit people say about hearing the smile over the line is really true. "Listen, buddy, I can't leave you by yourself. I'll just wait out here until your mom comes back, okay?"

A loud bang hits the flimsy trailer door and I hope it's him sitting on the other side.

"What's the monster's name?" I attempt to sound as friendly as possible.

"Max."

"Strong name."

"He's huge. Like the Incredible Hulk."

"Green?"

"Yeah. With a red bandana and he can spin on his back."

I purse my lips. I think the kid's got the Incredible Hulk and Rafael the Teenage Mutant Ninja Turtle a little confused.

"Does he wear ripped purple pants?"

"How did you know?" He honestly sounds shocked and I hold back a chuckle.

"I'm a good guesser."

"He has friends, too. One can fly and the other can swing from webs."

"Does he love pizza?"

"Yeah." There's surprise in his tone once more.

"Does he live in the sewer?"

He laughs. "No, he lives with me."

"To protect you?" I lean against the railing of the stairway, propping my knees up, trying to reach the small amount of shade the trailer leaves me.

"Yeah." His voice shrinks and I'm glad to hear the calm back in his voice.

"Who are you?" a female voice snaps from the other direction.

I whip my head around.

The boy might be calm, but his mom sure as hell isn't.

I swear she's heaving for breath like she's about to breathe fire and if I concentrated hard I bet I'd hear the echo of her beating heart. Quickly, I stand, running my hands down the length of my slacks.

"Hey, I'm Vance Rose. I believe you spoke to Jagger Kale?" I shove my hands in my pockets to not reach out and touch her.

The sun gleams off the highlights in her auburn hair and it looks as if glitter is sprinkling down from the sky and onto her. Now, I'm no poet, nor a romantic on any front, but I can't deny that this woman is ten times more stunning in person than she is in her movies. Her figure is slender with the perfect ratio of hips to chest and her bright green eyes leave nothing to guesswork—everything she's feeling is right there on display.

Immediately, guilt causes my stomach to clench because I was the reason she was sent packing, especially the *why* of it all.

I study her face for any form of recognition as to who I am. There's no way for her to know me by my real name, but I couldn't be one hundred percent sure.

She steps past me onto the stairs of the trailer.

"I heard you had a script?" Her voice is clipped and she barely offers me a passing glance as she opens the trailer door.

"Yes, the investor loves your work and wants you to sign on." I move to follow but the door slams in my face.

*What's with this family?*

"Payne!" she yells.

"Mommy!"

I turn the knob and peek my head in. The kid's now smiling face tells me my chances are good I won't be risking a concussion a third time.

"Where's Mary?" she asks her son while disposing of her bag on the floor. Payne picks up a nearby sword and runs toward me.

I pick him up under his arms and fly him around the room, effectively dodging his aim.

"She left," Payne says when I set him down. He continues trying to stab me with his play sword as I sidestep a couple of jabs.

"Was that the nanny?" I ask.

She narrows her eyes at me but doesn't answer.

Seriously, this chick's got an attitude usually earned by the forty-plus crowd of female actors who are past their heyday and can't find any more good roles to play.

"Let me guess." Her gaze moves from me to Payne. "What did you do?" Her hands land on her thin hips, her red lips puckered in the direction of the now innocent-looking little boy.

"Nothing." He jams the sword into my stomach and shit, that hurts.

I bellow and keel over.

"I'm sorry." Layla walks over and places her hand on my shoulder. "Are you okay?"

"Max will get him next," Payne says in a deep, mean-sounding voice.

"Stop it with Max. We talked about the invisible monsters thing." Her hand moves off me to her son and she pulls him down the short hallway. "I'll be right back."

They're in the back room but I overhear every word between them—her dictating how he should act and his consistent whining of, "But, Mom…"

She returns minutes later, minus Payne. Who, I might add, seems like a pain in the ass so it seems he was named appropriately.

"I'm so sorry." She sighs and pulls her long, auburn hair into a ponytail and sits down on the thinly cushioned couch beside me. "Did you want something to drink?" Her body shifts forward and is half up off the couch when my hand lands on her thigh to stop her.

Her eyes narrow on my hand and I quickly retract it, feeling like a creep. "Sorry."

She eases back down onto the most uncomfortable couch ever built.

"I hope you aren't some sleazy scriptwriter who wants me to practice the sex scenes with him on his casting couch." She laughs and the sound is almost musical. For some unknown reason my heart sputters over a couple of beats.

"Nah, just the kissing ones." I keep my face stone cold and her laughter slowly stops until I smile and shake my head.

She picks up right where she left off and this time it's her touching my shoulder. But I don't shake her off. I like the way it feels. Too much.

She rises from the couch again and I watch her ass sway as she walks the short distance to the mini-fridge.

Christ, I'm such an asshole—I'm visualizing her naked. As if I am that guy who's more interested in getting her spread-eagle on the casting couch than what her talent can add to my film.

"Water?" she asks over her shoulder.

I shake my head, admiring the curve of her body in the yoga pants plastered to her skin.

"Mommy!" The door at the back of the trailer opens and her head whips in that direction.

Payne stands in the doorway, his lips turned down in a frown.

"Go back in there, Payne." She points back in the room and the little boy's gaze moves to me. "Nope. You'll get no sympathy from me, young man. *Another* nanny gone. You need to learn how to behave."

Payne's chest heaves with a breath and he circles around, his shoulders shake and he slowly disappears in the room, slamming the door behind him.

Layla's chin drops forward to her chest and she inhales a deep breath before releasing it. But when she looks back up at me her face is masked with confidence.

"Let's talk about that script." She cracks open her water bottle and sits down on the couch again.

I wait a few seconds before I start in on my pitch. "It's about a couple on the run. Outlaws." I toss the script on the seat cushion between us. "You'd be playing Melanie."

She picks it up, and I notice her fingernails are perfectly polished in a shade not unlike the color of sand. It must be natural because I bet whatever role she's in, the audience isn't too focused in on her hands. Not with all the other assets she's got going for her.

"And who would be"—she thumbs through the script for a second—"Joseph?"

"If I said Ryan Gosling would you take the part?"

She focuses in on me for an uncomfortable beat before she shakes her head. "No, I like Eva. I'm rooting for them." She shuts the script and sips her water. Damn. I realize now that she must have wiped her lipstick off when she was in the back with Payne because they're pink now with a gloss of water over them and totally kissable. To the point of distraction.

*Get your shit together, man.*

I clear my throat. "Rooting for them?"

"Yeah, you know, because no relationships work in this industry. I think they might have what it takes though."

"And what is that?"

She stands and I follow her, ready to drink a cold water to cool the heat my body is generating in her presence. Opening the fridge, she hands me a water like she knew what I was going after.

"Thanks."

She nods, opening a pantry that barely has anything in it except animal crackers and raisins. I guess Payne must've nabbed the last granola bar to use as a weapon.

"You know, the magic." She picks up a small box of raisins, holds them up to me in question.

"No, thanks."

She shrugs and opens the box.

"Magic?"

She purses her lips and rolls her eyes. "Men," she says with a shake of her head. "The magic that keeps a relationship going. You know what L.A. is like... everyone is always screwing around with and then marrying their co-star. Most probably believe they've found their one and only. But then the next movie comes along with a hiatus from their loved one and next thing you know there's the next new, sexy co-star lying in their bed."

"I take it you don't sleep with co-stars?" I sit on the edge of the couch, drinking my water, watching her maneuver around the room, picking up toys and straightening up.

"Been there, done that, and got two great parting gifts for my troubles." She glances to the back bedroom. "No need to take any more gambles." Her nose scrunches up and she shakes her head.

"So you'll stay celibate for the rest of your life?" I ask with a chuckle.

*Shit. I can't believe I said that out loud. Real professional, asshole.*

Lifting her head from digging out a toy out from under the table, she blows a loose strand of hair from her vision.

"My hand and some electronics do a better job anyway." She shrugs a shoulder again.

"You can't be serious." My gaze roams over her body. Bad move. My dick was already at half-chub when I first saw her and now it's approaching full mast. My pants constrict in the crotch area and I shift to try to hide the obvious.

"Hell, yeah, I'm serious." Before I can argue, she raises her hand in the air to stop me from speaking. "Don't. I've heard it a million times."

"That I'd show you how much better I am than your hand?" I laugh.

She doesn't. She raises her eyebrows. "Exactly."

I'm helpless to stop my egotistical smirk from emerging. "Fair enough. I'll leave the details of my nine-inch pleasure pole to myself."

Her eyes widen and she instinctively glances at my crotch. When she reaches my eyes again, I raise an eyebrow.

"Payne, come on out." Her voice is more constricted than it was moments before, as if she's speaking around a giant lump in her throat.

The kid comes out of the room, his arms crossed over his chest and his head down.

"Thanks for coming by. I'll make sure to read the script over and get back to you this week."

Payne leans against the counter, glancing over at me.

*Shit, I've fucked this up.* "I was joking," I assure her.

She laughs. "I figured. I mean..." She widens her eyes at me.

"I wasn't joking about the nine."

Her face flushes and her gaze shoots to Payne.

*Shit, the kid.* I'm not used to being around innocent ears.

I hold my fist out to Payne, who blatantly ignores me, so I tuck my hand in the pocket of my pants.

"Well, that's information I don't really need to make a decision about whether or not I'm going to take the role." Her hands land on my shoulders and she spins me around until I'm facing the door. "Good evening, Mr. Rose."

Having no choice, I turn the doorknob. "Hope to hear from you soon, Miss Andrews." I circle back around. "Nice to meet you and your monster, Payne."

He stays mute.

"Well, then."

"He's just tired." Layla makes an excuse for him, while she's practically at my back until I start down the stairs. "Bye."

I swivel around to say goodbye, but the trailer door is already shut.

It seems pretty clear to me that Layla doesn't think there's much I can offer her—nine inches or not.

**4**

## Layla

The trailer door shuts and I wish I could pour my bottle of water over my head.

Vance Rose is one hell of a guy. It's no joke that there's a good-looking guy on every street corner in L.A. Hell, usually they're clustered together like they all belong to the same hive or something. But Vance Rose has dimples that make me want to swoon like a schoolgirl, hair I want to push my fingers through and a tall, lean build I'm itching to climb like a tree and wrap my legs around. And I haven't climbed a tree in a long damn time. Or had wood between my legs in almost as long, but that's another story.

"Mom!" Payne screams my name even though I'm right beside him and I snap out of the daydream of what I'd do to Vance if I was a single girl with next to no responsibilities, rather than a soon-to-be-divorced mom of two.

"I have to call the nanny service, honey. Can you give Mommy some privacy and go back into that room again?"

"You just told me to come out," he whines.

*I did. Why was that again?*

*God, I think I might be close to losing it.*

Oh, right, with the whole nine-inch comment from Vance I feared I'd prowl over to him on my hands and knees and unzip his fly in order to find out if his dick is as gorgeous as he is. The drought has been a long one and if someone doesn't water my little patch of grass soon I fear there'll be no saving it from becoming a wasteland.

"I forgot I had to make a few calls. Then we'll go get Via and head home."

I ruffle his blond hair and he shakes his head, but listens to me, sulking the whole way back to the bedroom. If only I could figure out why I'm the only one he listens to, that alone would solve a huge part of my problem. At least my childcare one.

I feel terrible at how much time he has to spend in this small trailer. His dad is off shooting on location—not that it would even matter. It's not like I can see my soon-to-be ex Carver stepping up in that regard. But Payne should be out riding his bike, playing with his friends, going to the zoo.

"How about we stop at Toys 'R' Us on the way?" I call out as he's readying to close the door.

He spins around, his eyes lighting up with happiness.

*Sue me, I bribe my kid.*

"Yay! Thanks, Mom." He rushes at me, knocking me off balance with the force of his hug.

Yeah, there's nothing better than this feeling of love from your child.

"You're welcome. Now, just give me a few minutes while I make some calls."

He nods and then runs into the room, shutting the door behind him.

Grabbing my phone from the counter, I dial up the nanny service I've been using for almost a year.

"Miss Andrews," Constance, the owner, answers and I know it's not a good sign.

"Hi, Constance. Mary left Payne in the care of a stranger. A *male* stranger." My voice has a bite of anger that's well deserved, but I attempt to keep it in check because at this point I'm at her mercy.

"She called. I'm so sorry, Miss Andrews. She's been terminated from the company."

The fight in me dies, since heads have already rolled. I need to focus on a solution to my problem now.

"That's good. Constance, I'm in the middle of filming, I need someone for at least three more weeks."

Her breath flows out over the phone. "Miss Andrews..."

"I know. I've been through a lot of nannies, but Payne promises to behave himself going forward." I sit down on the couch, running my thumb over the spine of the script. Very few have come my way for leading roles and those that have, have been abysmal. Normally my agent wouldn't have even mentioned this one to me since no one has ever heard of Vance Rose before, but Jagger Kale called him and asked if the writer could meet with me directly. If Jagger hadn't made that phone call our little meeting would never have happened, but he's not known to attach himself to useless endeavors and so I figured it was worth a few minutes of my time.

"Miss Andrews, I have no one left."

"No one?" I question in disbelief. Surely there's a recent graduate who needs a job? An empty-nester eager to fill her day?

"No one. You've had every one of my employees. I'm expecting another rush this summer, but in the meantime, I can't help you out." Her voice is pained so I think she may feel bad for me, but nonetheless, she could be lying.

"I'm desperate. I'll pay more than the usual."

"Miss Andrews, it's not about payment or the fact that Payne is one of our more... energetic children."

She's sweet, referring to Payne as energetic. He's basically a modern-day version of Dennis the Menace. If only I could find his Mr. Wilson.

"We just don't have the staff right now. I'm sorry."

My shoulders sink and I stare at the bedroom door. The best thing to happen to my life is also the worst thing to happen to my career. It's a horrible truth of working in showbiz and having children with a man who never lets them affect *his* career.

"Thanks, Constance. I'll figure something out, but please put me on the list for the next available nanny."

"Of course, Miss Andrews. You'll be one of the first ones I call."

"*The* first?" I clarify.

"Yes, Miss Andrews."

"I'll be the first?"

"Yes, one of. You aren't my only client."

And here I thought this conversation was going semi-okay. I know now that this woman isn't going to call me back. I'm probably last on the list of firsts.

"I know, but I may be a tad more desperate."

She laughs, and I can't help but think it sounds empty and uncaring now.

"I promise, Miss Andrews, your number is on speed dial."

For more than just one reason.

"Thank you, Constance."

"Of course, Miss Andrews. Good luck on finding someone and I'll be in touch."

We hang up and my head falls back to the hard cushion of the couch.

Damn it. Where the hell am I going to find a nanny?

———

Toys 'R' Us is its usual chaotic scene. Kids are whining in every aisle and every parent looks like they're on their last sane nerve.

"Let's make this quick," I remind Payne as he skips along the rows, searching out his favorite area.

We round the corner and he doesn't pause before heading right for the tented castle. Needing to get off my feet, I plop down on a queen's chair and allow my hand to hold up my head.

"I'm the knight." Payne's voice wakes me up from my comatose state.

"Payne." I shoot him a silent warning, my eyes veering over to the father whose attention is now on the fantasy tent in the middle of the play zone. Usually I can relax for a while before he's fighting with another kid about whose castle it is.

Is my son spoiled? Yes.

Is it my fault? Probably.

I'm not proud of that fact.

"You can't have the sword, it's mine." Payne's mean voice echoes out of the tent and the father peeks his head in only to usher his child out.

"I'm sorry." I stand to my feet. "Payne, honey, time to go."

The man holds his—whoa—son's hand. A son who is probably twice the size of Payne. My son knows no fear.

"It's okay. We've been here for a while." The father shoots me a crooked smile and his gaze falls down my body and then back up.

*One. Two. Three.*

He leans forward. "Are you Layla Andrews?" he whispers. At least he's not one of those people who scream and pull their phone out for a picture.

"I am." I soften my own tone with the hopes he doesn't try to sell a story about Layla Andrew's son accosting his child to the tabloids.

"I thought so."

The boy wrangles out of his dad's hold and flies back into the tent.

NOOOO.

"I'm Zeke Donner." The man holds out his hand and I shake it absentmindedly, my mind too occupied with what Payne could be doing to his poor son inside that tent.

"Hello."

"May I say, you're so much prettier than the magazines make you look." His green eyes sparkle and although I'm not looking for love, he seems like a decent guy.

A regular guy dressed in jeans and a t-shirt who actually takes care of his child. There's something sexy about a man who takes charge of his responsibilities.

"Yeah, well, they seem to have a way of finding me on those mornings I'm just running out for coffee and donuts." I laugh.

His eyes fixate on my mouth, but he doesn't laugh with me.

"This probably seems crazy, but how about dinner?" He extends his arm so his long-sleeved t-shirt rises when he takes a glance at his watch. "I know my son is going to be throwing himself on the ground soon." A deep chuckle leaves his throat and before I can politely decline, Payne and his boy run out of the tent.

Zeke's son has the sword and a shield strapped to his chest. At least he has protection.

"Yeah. Let's go to the King's Quarters," Payne says and I glance to the dad, whose eyes are filled with hope.

"The King's Quarters?" The other boy's shoulders fall. "I want to go to Playzone. The ball pit." His green eyes that match his father's stare up, as though he's saying, *Do not make me go to the King's Quarters.*

Zeke pats his son on the head. "We'll go to Playzone tomorrow."

The kid's eyes dig giant craters into the side of Payne's head. I cover it to protect Payne on the off chance he has powers.

Yeah, I've been in the movie business way too long.

"After you." Zeke's hand extends out in front of us.

Payne skips along the path and I slow my footsteps, waiting for Zeke to catch up to me. "I hate to decline, but I have a million things to do."

He stuffs his hands into his pockets. "Miles, catch up to Payne, okay?" He nudges his son forward and Miles runs after Payne. The two start playing a video game up ahead seconds later.

Keeping an eye on him, I continue on. "Maybe we could meet up—"

His hand lands on my arm and I freeze in place. The calloused palm of a man on my bare skin is a foreign feeling these days.

"Sorry." He retracts his hand and I blow out a breath. It was a friendly, not a creepy gesture and I shouldn't be making this man feel like a leper.

I'm a grown woman. I can date. Zeke seems nice, and why not dinner? The kids can play and I can have an adult conversation while I eat for once. Surely the script can wait until tomorrow.

"No, I'm sorry. Dinner sounds great." I smile, toothier than usual, with the hope it counteracts the bitchy cold shoulder I just gave him.

"No need to apologize. I'm not sure what I did to change your mind, but I'm glad you did." His footsteps pause by the kids.

"Come on, Payne," I say. He glances back but continues to play the game.

"Miles, let's go. Pizza." Zeke's voice is low but authoritative.

Miles places the remote on the game console and walks back to his dad.

"Payne," I say sweetly and he glances back at me. I widen my eyes and then he does what Miles did seconds earlier. Always walking that line, this one.

The four of us leave Toys 'R' Us without a toy by some miracle, but I should have known my luck would run out there.

By the time the sliding doors of the store open to the parking lot, two cameramen are outside and the flashes of their cameras blind me. I wince and pick up Payne. He knows the drill. Head in the crook of my neck and never look up unless absolutely necessary.

Zeke wraps his arm around my shoulders, guiding us to the parking lot. His gesture isn't possessive. I take it more as him being decent and knowing how intrusive this all must feel—especially with my child present.

But it's not going to appear as innocent as it is and this will all end in horrible headlines. Headlines that will make Carver flip.

"I think we'll have to postpone that dinner," I mumble, hoping the paparazzi are far enough away they can't hear me.

"No. It's fine."

I finally look from the black pavement to see Miles in his arms, mimicking the same position as Payne, except his chin is propped up on his dad's shoulder and he's staring at the cameras.

"Sorry, Zeke. Thank you." I unlock our car with my key fob, open the driver's door and Payne knowingly crawls through the middle opening, strapping himself into his car seat.

We worked on that stunt for an hour, since it's faster than

me strapping him in and then rounding the car. It lessens the chance of embarrassing shots of my dress flying up, or my thong poking out of the top of my jeans, or me losing my temper on the paps when they have a camera shoved in my almost five-year-old's face.

Zeke and Miles stand outside my car and the disappointment etched on both of their faces is a look I'm all too familiar with, but it's better this way. I'm sure there's a reason he's a single dad. If he even is. God, I hope he's not married. That's all I need.

I shake my head. This is the best for everyone. Who was I to think I could meet a normal everyday guy? I press the button to start my SUV and wave before driving away.

**5**

## Layla

Three cups of coffee might be too much, but my eyes are permanent bloodshot slits. The all-nighter was worth it though. Vance Rose has skills and the fact that he's willing to have me play the snarky lead, the girlfriend of a pathological liar who convinces her to travel across the United States stealing from people and businesses alike, brings a giddiness that I don't usually have when I'm given a script.

I mean, my current role as the sweet best friend who's always home when the lead actress returns from bedding the hero is my typecast role. Whether it's five o'clock or ten o'clock, I'm there being the third wheel in a romantic comedy. Always sweet. Always innocent. Just like the roles I played my entire childhood.

Vance scribbled his number on the script before he left yesterday, but it's only seven in the morning. Could he be the type who wakes up early to work out? I wouldn't doubt it with the way his clothes hugged his body yesterday. Or maybe he stays out all night partying and sleeps half the day away. For some reason I find myself disappointed at that thought.

Flipping my phone over and over again, I chew on the inside of my cheek. I have to get rid of this ridiculous smile, but this could be the role that changes my pigeon-holed path in this industry. So long romantic comedies and hello dramas! My gaze lingers on the room around me. Payne's toys piled in the corner. Via's hair bow and sippy cup from yesterday lying on the table. My smile fades because I remember that I don't have a nanny to watch Payne for the next three weeks—or this next film.

Via can continue to go to daycare, but Payne was kicked out two months ago. I was going to take a break after this role and spend time with the kids before Payne starts kindergarten. I should delay this part in Vance's film, pass on it, but God, it's my breakthrough role, I'm positive. I can feel it. Doing this film will change my life for the better.

Without thinking of repercussions, I look into the family room to make sure Via is still playing there and then flip my phone around, thumb through my contacts and click the call button.

It rings. And rings.

My fingers caress the script. Such magnificent work.

"Hello?" Carver answers and bile rises in my throat like it does every time I hear my soon-to-be ex-husband's voice.

"Carver."

"Layla? Are Payne and Via okay?" His tone is more inquisitive than worried.

"Is this the part where you act like a caring father?"

Sue me, okay? He might pay his child support but he has pretty much zero presence in their day-to-day lives.

"So, this is how the conversation is going to go?" I hear the flick of his lighter.

"Still smoking?"

The sound of him exhaling sounds through the receiver and I realize I don't really need an answer.

"Why are you calling?" he snaps.

An empty and hollow laugh leaves my mouth. "Funny thing. I decided it's time you actually care about and for your kids."

He sighs. "Layla, I gotta get back on set. What's going on?"

"I have a part that I need you to come home for. I'm tapping out and you need to tap in."

"Why are we talking boxing lingo?" Another inhale.

"Carver, you need to come back. When is your movie done filming?"

He sighs again. "I'm done here next week, but I got another offer for an upcoming film another actor dropped out of because he had to go to rehab. I'll be in Florida for eight weeks."

My hand slams down on the table. "Carver, I need your help here."

"Get a nanny."

My teeth grind together and I ball my hands into fists. "Do you think I haven't tried that? He's gone through six."

"Well, surely there are more than six nannies in all of LA. I mean, no one really watches their kids themselves in that city."

"Six this *week*. He went through two in one day." I hear the creak of the hardwood floors behind me and my shoulders fall.

I turn to see Payne standing there in his ninja pajamas, wearing a Hulk mask. Although I can't see his eyes, he's not his usual energetic self this morning. I hold my arm out for him to come to me.

"Do you want to talk to Payne? He just woke up."

I hear the director in the background, but Carver's the lead, surely he can ask them to hold on a second.

"I'll call tonight, I gotta go."

The phone clicks in my ear and he's already gone.

Payne crawls into my lap and lays his head on my shoulder.

"Was that Daddy?" he asks, way too used to the drill.

"Yeah, he's going to call us back tonight," I say with false brightness.

His silence is evidence that we both know he won't.

"I'm sorry, Mommy," he whispers.

I hold him closer. I knew he heard me.

"I know, sweetie. Do you think you could try to be better for the nannies from now on? If I can find one?"

He draws back from me, his soft brown eyes still sleepy. "Yeah."

I inhale a deep breath. This is why he is the way he is. I can hardly discipline him when his father is a constant disappointment.

"Okay. How about some pancakes?" I pat his butt to get him to slide off me so I can make some breakfast and try to get Carver out of my head.

He walks to the family room, picking up the ball Via dropped and handing it over to her.

Fifteen minutes later, the smoke from the pancakes fills our entire downstairs. I spin the dial to off and push the skillet off the burner.

So much for getting Carver out of my head. He occupied it so much, I burned our entire breakfast.

"Mommy?" Payne comes in, his eyebrows raised.

"Want to go out to breakfast?"

He smiles and nods, runs off, screaming, "I'll go get dressed!"

Grabbing my phone, I text-message Vance. I need to secure our future because Lord knows I'm the only parent who's going to. A leading role will surely produce more offers and then maybe I can hire a full-time live-in nanny. It'll be hard in the moment, but best for the three of us in the future.

**Me:** *Hi. This is Layla Andrews. I finished the script last night. I'd love to meet to talk it over. I'm heading out to breakfast with my kids. Call me whenever you wake up.*

My thumb hovers over the send button.
*Why am I nervous?*
I click send before second-guessing myself any further.
Three dots appear below my message immediately.

**Vance:** *Kids? As in plural?*
**Me:** *Yes, I have Payne and Via, an eighteen-month-old. Is that a problem?*
**Vance:** *If I say yes, I'd be sued.*

WELL, his response doesn't exactly scream 'your kids are welcome on set with you,' now does it?

**Vance:** *BTW, I've been up since six. Where are you going for breakfast?*

A smile plays on my lips and I bite the inside of my cheek again.

**Me:** *We're going to Pancake Express. You must work out or something if you're up that early.*

**Vance:** *Are you imagining me working out? And you haven't even seen my abs yet. Kinky. I like it.*

I smile to myself. This man is such a flirt. I'm sure he

means nothing by it, he's this way with everyone, yet I can't help the way my breathing gets shallow when he does.

**Vance:** *Pancake Express tastes like cardboard. Meet me at Yolk Me.*

A third text comes through with the address of Yolk Me and my stomach flips a few times at the thought of seeing him again.

I pick up Via and walk upstairs to my bedroom and end up getting a little too done up for breakfast, telling myself it's because I want the part and not the man.

———

AFTER DROPPING Via off at daycare, because there's no way I'll be able to have a conversation with Vance while my eighteen-month-old is grabbing at every single item on the table, Payne and I enter Yolk Me. It has a hipster vibe with different seating arrangements for every table and is a far cry from Pancake Express, where your legs stick to the vinyl booths. But Pancake Express is simple. Twenty different kinds of pancakes. If you want eggs, you go somewhere else. I secretly hope Yolk Me isn't some organic vegan restaurant with tofu and sprouts because I'll have a screaming kid on my hands.

Waiting by the hostess stand, I'm surprised on how empty the restaurant is, especially with it being nine in the morning. Yeah, it's middle of the week, but this is LA, not some small town in the middle of the Nebraska cornfields.

"Did you get a table yet?" Vance approaches from behind and shivers run up my spine at the sound of his deep voice.

Does this guy have some love potion splashed all over him that intoxicates me every time he's near? I practically turn into an emoji with two hearts for eyes.

"Not yet. I guess there's too many customers, the hostess can't keep up."

One side of his mouth tips up in the most mouth-watering smirk until he focuses on Payne at my side, who surprisingly seems as mesmerized by this man as me.

"Hey, Payne. Good morning." He holds his hand up for a high-five, and Payne smacks it. "Come on, you can do better than that."

Payne's lips curl at the corners and he's wearing the same expression he gives the nannies when they first walk through the door, as if he's sussing them out. He pulls his arm back like he's about to throw a ball and then smacks his hand as hard as he can against Vance's.

The slap echoes in the restaurant, and surprise, surprise, it garners the attention of the hostess and she finally shows up.

"Sorry," I mumble as Vance shakes his hand from the force of a four-year-old.

"You know, I'd never want to run into you in a dark alley." He shakes his head at Payne.

"Payne's working on his communication skills." I smile and Vance's head falls back into laughter.

"Good luck with that." Then his eyes set on the hostess. "Three or four?" He turns to me. "Where's your son, daughter?"

"Daughter. Via is at daycare."

Small wrinkles appear on his forehead but he holds three fingers up for the hostess without comment.

"Mommy, Mommy, Mommy." Payne tugs on my sleeve. "They have some games. Can I play? Please, please, please."

"His communication skills seem fine to me," Vance says and slides into the booth.

I dig into my purse, but Vance hands him a five-dollar bill. "Go have fun."

Payne doesn't even wait before he scurries toward the line

of games, or the money suckers, as I like to think of them. He'll be back in five minutes and all of Vance's money will be gone, mark my words.

As though Vance can hear my unspoken thoughts, he says, "The games are set up so that kids win no matter what. I picked this place because they have great food, but they're kid-friendly." He lifts the coffee the hostess poured to his lips.

"How did you know Payne would be with me?" I grab two Stevias and pour them into my coffee.

"Well, I witnessed the nanny running away yesterday." He raises his eyebrows and the brown depths of his eyes remind me of melted chocolate. And who doesn't like chocolate?

"Not exactly the best first impression." Embarrassment colors my face and the skin on my cheeks heats, feeling almost as if I'm lying out sunbathing on a hot summer day.

His hands wrap around his mug and he glances over to Payne, who is making the claw fall into the bin of stuffies over and over again. I know my child—he won't relent until he gets whatever he has his eye on. "I've never been a believer in that phrase about not making a bad first impression."

"No?"

He shakes his head. "As you get to know people, that's the impression that matters. People tend to be fake when you first meet them. Even more so in L.A. Like you, for instance."

"Me?" My eyes bulge out of my head and I wait for him to continue. I've never been the fake person who is nice when cameras are around and a demanding bitch when they aren't.

"I'm sure people are sweet as pie to you when they first meet you. You're a celebrity, but as time goes by, you see what they're really after."

"Psychology one-on-one from Vance Rose?" I sip my coffee and he chuckles.

"More like ramblings from Vance Rose. Most of them don't even make sense."

"Well, that one did. I tend to pull back in relationships. Being as young as I was when my career started... I have a limited list of people I'd consider true friends."

Even with the words out of my mouth, I can't help but feel like a loser. I have one good girlfriend and she lives back home in Kentucky.

"Quality more than quantity. I like it." He runs his fingers through his hair and the waves settle in a messy look that's good on him.

"Well." I pull out the script. "I love the part. I was up all night reading it. I know you said an investor wanted me, but since you wrote this, I want to know if *you* see me in this role."

He shifts in his seat, stares over to Payne once more and then to the counter. Wow. His non-verbal cues are screaming his answer as if it were plastered in flashing, neon lights around the restaurant.

"Is that a no?" I ask, suddenly feeling as insecure as I did when I went for my first audition as a child.

"No, I'm not sure I ever thought about an actress for it. I figured when we did auditions, I'd see it, but the investor wants you. So here we are." He shrugs.

"Not exactly a ringing endorsement. You're familiar with my work?"

"I am." He lifts his hand to flag down the waitress, obviously wanting to escape this conversation. "We should order. I'm sure your son is hungry."

The waitress listens and takes out her pad and pen. Although she looks to Vance first, he gestures for me to order first.

"He'll have a milk and the blueberry pancakes. I'll have an egg white omelet with spinach."

The waitress nods.

"That's it? No toast or pancakes?"

Even though I was going to order pancakes at Pancake Express, and I've already promised myself I'd run on the treadmill tonight after the kids went to bed, this man holds my future in his hands with this role and I want him to know I have excellent willpower and won't gain weight.

"No." I shake my head.

He waits for a second and then looks up to the waitress. "I'll have the multigrain pancakes with strawberries, and can you bring her a German oven pancake?"

The waitress stuffs her pad and pen back in her apron. "Be right back."

"I'm not going to eat the pancake," I say.

A small smirk plays on his lips. "One bite?"

I shake my head. "We'll see." I roll my eyes. We both know I'll be eating it. "So, you really need me to do the film?"

He swallows down his sip of coffee. "Yeah, I don't think I've hidden the fact that if I don't have you, my script doesn't sell. No Layla, no money to make the film."

"So we can bargain?" I thought long and hard about this conversation on the ride over. How am I going to do this?

"Well, I don't have a ton to offer you. The film won't have a huge budget, but I'll make sure it's fair and if it does well we can probably negotiate more on the back end."

I shake my head. "I'm not looking for more money. What I need isn't really about money."

He tilts his head and a sour look crosses his face before he shoots me what I assume is his fake smile. I haven't seen that one yet. I should spit it out.

"As far as amenities, you can give me a list and I'll make sure it's all in your trailer during shooting. We can get you set up with transportation if you'd like. I won't have anything until I talk with the investor, but that's not going to happen until you agree."

I have to admit this level of power is intoxicating. I've

never been on the end of negotiations where I held all the cards.

"No." I shake my head. "My needs are more immediate."

His face distorts and he looks over to Payne, who is trying to get his head into the prize slot of the game.

"Shit." Vance slides out from the booth and runs over to my son.

They say timing is everything and as far as these things go, Payne's isn't the best given what I have to ask Vance.

**6**

## Layla

Vance has one hand in the toy exit compartment by the time I reach them. Payne's head pops out, but his arm is still stuck.

"What were you thinking?" I shriek. Okay, my voice might be on the cusp of a scream.

"I want the poop emoji." Payne winces and Vance tries to twist his arm to get it out.

"Did you think you could squeeze your entire body in there?"

I'm still in disbelief and completely mortified that Payne went this far for a stuffed animal that I could buy at Walgreens for a few bucks.

"I'm not that big."

Vance glances over to me and he's probably thinking to himself, *Save up for college, lady, because there'll be no scholarships here.* Then he focuses on helping my son escape.

"That hurts!" Payne yells.

"He's trying to help you." My teeth are clenched as I give him my best 'shut up and be polite' expression, hoping that this one time he understands.

"Ouch." Payne's voice moves down an octave.

"Sorry, buddy, I think I almost have it." Vance looks to the waitress who's now joined the show. "Can you get us a bag of ice?"

I look over my shoulder and see her scrambling toward the kitchen.

Vance's gaze locks with mine. "He'll be fine, just a little sore." A smile appears on his face and in that moment, my body relaxes.

Payne pulls his arm through the hole and I'm prepared for him to hug me, tell me how scared he was, but of course that doesn't happen. Instead Vance wraps his one good arm around Payne and sits next to him as the waitress hands Vance the bag of ice.

My ass falls down to rest on my heels and I watch the display of affection Vance has for a kid who isn't his. A kid who in all honesty probably annoys the shit out of him.

"It's red, but you're fine. Next time, come and get me." Vance winks at Payne.

"What would you do?" Payne asks, the corners of his lips tipped up.

"I'll win it for you."

"How?"

I stay silent, enjoying the conversation happening between them. It's nothing of importance. Vance isn't telling Payne how to behave. Not reprimanding him for something. He's just talking to him and Payne's actually responding.

"Let me show you." Vance positions his hand under Payne's arm and helps him up. "Ready?" Vance asks Payne.

Payne nods enthusiastically.

Vance presses the buttons on the machine, arranging the crane. "What do you think, Payne? Back further?" Vance asks.

Payne moves to the side and I doubt he even really knows what he's talking about. "Back."

Vance presses the button and the crane hardly moves. He looks back at me and winks. Giddiness floods my stomach and I almost want to press my face against the glass like Payne's. Can he get the poop emoji?

"It's piled in there pretty good," I say.

Vance and Payne's heads whip in my direction and I back up with my hands in the air.

"No doubters allowed." Vance turns to Payne. "Close your eyes when we press the button, okay?"

Payne nods his head up and down. "Can I press it?"

"Sure." Vance holds out his arm, allowing Payne to squeeze between the machine and his chest. "One. Two. Close your eyes."

Payne giggles. Actually giggles as his finger hovers over the button.

"Three."

Payne presses the button and what feels like pride races through me because he actually listened to someone else's instructions. Most days, he would have probably just pressed the button on one.

I watch the crane fall down with child-like excitement.

"Layla, tell us what's happening," Vance says, his gorgeous caramel eyes hidden under his eyelids.

"The crane is going down... it's widening now and falling into the stuffed animals."

"Cross your fingers, Payne." Vance holds up his own hands with his fingers crossed. Payne does the same thing, although he struggles with getting the middle finger over the pointer. "Keep going," Vance urges.

"It's pulling back up now. Seriously?" The poop emoji is in the grasp of the crane.

"What? What is it, Mommy?" Payne must actually have his eyes shut. Unbelievable.

The stuffed animal drops into the toy compartment.

"Open your eyes and look in the drop area."

Payne bends down and digs his hand into the drop box.

Vance opens his eyes, looking to me first, silently asking me if they won. I keep my expression as neutral as possible.

"You're awesome." Payne holds up the poop emoji and Vance picks him up, spinning him around the small restaurant.

"Nah, you're awesome. You pressed the button."

Payne smiles over at me, holding the stuffed animal in his hands.

"Now it's time to eat," I say.

"No. Let's do it again," Payne whines and I sigh. I knew this new attitude of his would be short-lived.

"You need to refuel first." Vance drops him to the ground and holds his arm out toward the table.

I stand there, watching the two of them venture off to the table. Payne slides into my side of the booth while Vance sits on his own. They're talking about emojis and which one is their favorite. My eyes won't turn away but my feet won't move either.

"Are you joining us?" Vance turns around and asks.

I nod, setting one foot in front of the other. I've never seen Payne have a conversation and be so well-behaved with another adult.

Sitting down, I take my fork and knife to cut up his blueberry pancakes.

"What's your favorite emoji, Mommy?"

"Let's guess," Vance says and Payne's eyes light up. "Anger?"

I narrow my eyes to a smiling Vance.

"Winks?" Payne asks.

Truthfully, I'm twenty-eight years old. I don't really have a favorite emoji and since I don't have very many friends who I text on a consistent basis, there's no emoji I use more than others.

"Yeah." I smile to my son, pouring syrup over his pancakes.

"I would have thought you'd be more of a face with rolling eyes emoji," Vance says with a straight face, taking a bite of his pancakes.

I stare at him blankly.

"Oh, I think I'm seeing the unamused emoji face right now." Vance points with his fork at me and Payne peeks over to see.

"It's a smirking emoji face now," Vance says.

My lips start turning up even though I do my best to keep them straight.

"There we go. You've got a grinning emoji face now."

I shake my head, keeping my eyes focused down on my omelet.

"Payne, is your mom ticklish?"

Payne's fork drops on his plate, in the syrup of course. His fingers start digging into my ribcage, not at all like tickling, more like tiny little daggers, but it's his way.

"Keep going. She's almost to a grinning emoji with smiling eyes face."

I lose all control of my face at that point and start laughing, tickling Payne back.

"You're talented, buddy. You got her to rolling on the floor laughing emoji."

Payne raises his arm up in the air and fist-pumps. "I'm awesome."

We both look at one another and laugh at his serious face.

"I think we should ask Vance why he knows so much about emojis," I say with a smile.

Vance places his fork down, wipes his mouth with his

napkin, and then holds his arms out. "Because I'm one cool guy."

Payne's smiling face and nodding head say he agrees and I can't pretend that I don't either.

———

ALL DURING BREAKFAST Vance tries to explain the different Ninja Turtles and superheroes to Payne, who keeps thinking Rafael must be a superhero. Eventually they agree to let the Turtles be superheroes, too.

I dig another five dollars out of my purse so that Payne can go back to the games. Vance and I need to finish our earlier conversation.

"Promise, no putting your hand in?" I hold the five dollars up in the air.

"Promise. I'll get Vance this time."

My gaze instinctively moves to Vance and then back to Payne. I hand him the money.

"I'm sorry, we're taking up your entire morning," I say.

He shakes his head, his hands wrapped around his coffee mug again. "I have nowhere to be. I already worked out."

I feel the heat rise up into my cheeks, thinking of our earlier texts. I'd have to be his mother not to notice his amazing body and the fact he works to get it tells me he goes after what he wants.

"Yeah, right." I grab another Splenda and rip it open, dumping it into my cup. "So, what were we talking about before my son tried to commit theft under a thousand?"

Vance picks up his coffee and leans back in the booth.

"You mentioned something about your immediate needs." He leans forward, his coffee mug hovering over the table. "Was that code that you want to practice some of the sex scenes?"

The scene in the story where the lead actress is perched up on a dresser in a sleazy motel and the lead has her legs open, eating her out while bags of cash and jewelry lie on the bed, comes to mind.

I swallow deeply, wishing he wouldn't affect me this much. Where's his professionalism? I should scold him for his demeanor, but for some reason I don't want to.

"No." My giddy schoolgirl voice rings out and he raises both eyebrows, relaxing into the booth once more. "I need a nanny."

"I'm sure there's some great agencies. Do you want me to see if I can find some references?"

I shake my head. "I have calls out but I'm back on set tomorrow. I need someone as soon as possible. The agencies will want to interview me and I'll have to interview them in return. I have no time for that. My parents live up in Napa and they're too busy starting a bed-and-breakfast to be bothered with my problems."

"Carver?" he asks, his words sounding like they're tainted with poison.

I shouldn't be surprised he knows my ex's name. Everyone knows everyone's business in this industry. "Filming."

"For how long?"

"Indefinitely."

His lips turn down. "So, what are you asking for, Layla?" His fingers clench harder around his coffee cup.

"Well, for me to agree to the part, I need a nanny." The napkin in my lap rips apart from the twisting of my fingers.

"A nanny?" Confusion paints all the features on his face.

"Or a manny, as it were?" I clarify, mentally crossing my fingers that this man can be a guardian angel in disguise and help to solve my problem.

## Vance

I heard wrong. Right? What the hell is a manny? And why does she think I'd be able to find her one?

"What do you need from me?" I ask.

The glimmer that's been in her eyes all morning dims and she sets her attention on where Payne is playing. There's a note of sadness in them that wasn't there before.

"The nanny service I use has no one else to send. Payne isn't a bad kid, he's just going through something right now. It's been hard with Carver gone."

Their split was big news last year, but like everything in LA, another story takes over the next day and it's old news. At the time I thought, *Another childhood romance crashes and burns.* Usual business around these parts. But seeing the pained look in Layla's eyes as she looks on to Payne, I can see I was a fool.

"Yeah, I heard. I'm sorry."

She's quick to shake her head, feigning nonchalance, but her body language says so much more.

"He's filming and I have no idea when he'll be back. Payne puts on a good front but I know he's confused over why

Carver hasn't returned. Why we haven't gone to visit him. I don't know if he's acting out for attention or what, but I have three weeks left of filming and no nanny."

I feel for the woman, I do, but I have no idea where to find a good nanny. Hell, when I was younger, it was the kid down the street. No one looked for twenty-four-hour help.

"There must be another service you can call."

She nods. "No, there is, it's just I have to apply and most reputable agencies don't just assign one to you like a package."

"So how can I help you on this then? You want me to conduct the interviews since you're busy?"

I'm afraid for this woman's sanity. I'm a thirty-four-year-old bachelor. What the hell do I know about what makes a good nanny?

"I was thinking you could do it," she says, sounding hopeful.

Now I know for sure something's wrong with her.

"Do what?" I raise a brow and take a sip of my coffee.

"Be his manny."

My coffee somehow takes a wrong turn into my windpipe. I start coughing and coffee spews out of my mouth. I beat on my chest for a second as my eyes water and eventually get my coughing fit under control. Reaching for a napkin to wipe up the mess dotting the table, I ask, "I'm sorry, his what?"

"You seem to like him and he responds well to you. Look at him now."

We both turn our heads, finding him hugging the poop emoji to himself. He almost looks angelic, but yesterday's demon eyes aren't forgotten. There's definitely a Jekyll to his Hyde.

"Layla, I want you to take the part. Half because of the investor and half because you seem really excited about the role and I think you could do a good job of it. But a nanny, or manny, I am not. Does he wear a diaper? I have no idea how to put those on, and I shouldn't be cleaning him up... down there."

She laughs and her perfectly bleached teeth glow like the sunshine on an early morning.

"He's been potty-trained since two and a half."

"Okay, but still. I'm not qualified."

"You wouldn't have the baby. I'd keep her in daycare. It would just be Payne and only until I could find something else. A week, tops." The desperation in her voice already has me caving.

"Look, I'm not your guy. I don't know the first thing about taking care of a four-year-old."

She reaches across the table and grips my hand in hers. "Please. I can't bail on this job when we're already halfway through filming. It'll make me look unprofessional, cost the studio money, and I'll never get another job again."

I shake my head. "Layla, I can't."

She releases my hands and slumps back against her seat. "But you stayed," she near-whispers.

I push my coffee aside, not needing any more caffeine to make me more anxious. My heart's already trying to catch up to the adrenaline pumping through my arteries. "Stayed?"

"You have to be a good guy. When the nanny left, you didn't pawn Payne off on someone else. You didn't come looking for me somewhere. You didn't even force him to open the door. You just sat outside and waited. He told me about how you talked to him through the door." She's smiling again, one that reminds me of someone reliving a fond memory.

"I might know enough not to leave a kid by himself, but I'll probably swear in front of him."

"He's heard it all. Just don't let him use them."

"I could lose him somewhere. I'm used to being by myself."

"Payne isn't a drifter. He sticks close to the hip."

"My apartment is full of glass and breakables."

"You can watch him at my place."

She smiles again and my gaze drifts to the counter.

"Are you going to give me an answer to every reason?"

She nods.

"So in order for you to take the part…"

"You need to be his manny."

"You'll be working on finding someone else?"

"Yep, and then I'll be sure to have someone before shooting starts on your film, too."

The waitress comes over with a coffee pot, but I decline nicely, whereas Layla takes another cup.

"You don't even know me," I say.

"My manager did a police check on you last night."

"You did a police check on me without asking?"

She smiles, placing her spoon on the shredded napkin on the table. "Of course. Do you think I'd let some weirdo watch my son?"

My heart rate picks up. Even though I know it would take an extensive background check to ever connect the two.

"One week, Layla, and I can't make any promises about how he'll be after that week. He could be swearing as much as a truck driver, hopped up on sugar, and have thumb callouses from video games."

She laughs like I'm kidding. "So that's a yes?" she asks, a contagious smile on her face.

"It's an 'I guess.' Under protest."

Her hands clap together and she bounces in her seat a little before calming back down.

"Thank you, Vance. I owe you." The sincerity in her voice tells me she means it.

"Just do one hell of a job on this film."

"I will. I promise. I'll text you my address. You're a lifesaver."

Then we sit in silence as I contemplate what I just agreed to and whether or not I even had a choice not to accept. I don't think so. Did I? I shouldn't have helped the kid with the toy. I shouldn't have put on that big-brother act, but I was trying to win Layla over so she'd take the part, not trying to apply for her nanny position.

I can handle anything for a week. Seven days. Easy-peasy. This kid thinks he's tough but I can be a drill sergeant if I have to be. If one of us is going to break, it isn't going to be me.

## 8

## Vance

"You're going to be her manny?" The questioning tone in Leo's voice makes me lose some of my earlier confidence. Could I really screw this kid up in a matter of days?.

"But she agreed to take on the role, right?" Jagger takes a bite of his taco.

"Yeah, she agreed." I push my plate away, for once not in the mood to eat.

Jagger and Leo went surfing this morning so I stopped here to meet up with them for lunch. Lucky for us, Heidi is off today, so we can have a conversation without Leo and I having to witness the endless flirting between her and Jagger.

"I don't get it. Why can't she find someone else?" Leo's still questioning why I would agree to something like this and I can't say I blame him, but I'm exhausted from talking about it and don't care to go into details.

"If he wants his film made, he needs to do whatever it takes to get her to accept the role. If the manny is her ultimatum, then being the manny is it." Jagger takes a quick swig of his beer and then points it in my direction. "Call me when you head to the park with the little guy, okay?" He winks over another mouthful of taco.

"So you can reap the benefits of my hard work? Hell, no. I'll be the one handing out my phone number to the ladies."

"Pfft," Leo says. "A kid has nothing on a dog, man. You should see all the flirting that happens when I take Cooper to the dog park."

We all laugh because we've all seen how his dog acts like a pussy magnet.

"It's just the boy? How old is he?" Leo asks. Forget the doggy spa and clothing line he owns—this guy should be on *60 Minutes* interviewing people.

"He's four. Layla has a daughter, too, but she's still really young, so she'll be in daycare." I take a sip of my beer, staring out into the ocean and letting the hypnotic vision of the waves rolling into shore over and over again relax me a bit.

I was on my way to join these guys when I got Layla's text this morning. I should've gone surfing instead of meeting her. It would have given her extra time to find a nanny.

"She has *two* kids? Isn't she like seventeen?" Leo's face distorts and I laugh at his lack of knowledge of the biz. The man spends most of his time sewing clothes for dogs.

"She's twenty-eight."

"Really?" His eyes bug out. "I guess I can't picture her as anything other than the little sister on that show she was on."

I nod and so does Jagger.

"*Growing Up Baxter*, right?" He snaps his fingers and points to me. "That's it. She still as hot as she was back then?"

"She's fucking gorgeous," Jagger says before I can answer and for some reason his response bothers me. "She was married to Carver Sterling."

"She was married to her brother?" The distaste on his face is clear.

Leave it to Leo.

"They're actors," I remind him.

He tilts his head and gives me the 'no shit' face. "They still played brother and sister for years. That's gross."

"You do know..." Jagger looks up at me and shakes his head. "Never mind."

"So you think she's gorgeous?" Leo throws his balled-up napkin on the plate and pushes it away from him.

"Jagger said that." I point to Jagger, but both their gazes land on me. "Jagger thinks the fifty-year-old librarian down the street is hot," I say with a laugh.

"She's a total MILF, dude," Jagger says. "Get your head out of your dog's ass for once and you might notice shit like that."

Leo rolls his eyes at Jagger and turns his attention to me. "So? Is she pretty?" He says 'pretty' with a childish tone and bats his eyes for emphasis.

"Yeah, she's pretty."

Jagger smiles and Leo leans forward on the table.

"You like her?" he asks.

I shrug. "She seems nice. Lives one crazy-ass life. Two kids, a soon-to-be ex-husband who doesn't give a shit. I kinda feel bad for her."

That's the truth. It was impossible not to notice the bags under her eyes no matter the amount of cover-up she'd put on, or the fact that her eyes were bloodshot and her movements all had a worn-out quality to them. She's permanently tired and half the reason I agreed to help her was to give the woman a break. I need her to be her best for my film.

"Uh-huh." Leo purses his lips, nodding his head. "You like her."

I throw my napkin at him, hitting him square on the forehead. "This isn't junior high."

My two friends look at one another. "He likes her," they say in unison.

"I'm out of here." I stand and tuck my chair back in.

"Going to get toys to impress the kid?" Leo asks.

"Conference call tomorrow at ten with the investor." Jagger wipes his face and disposes of his napkin on his plate, letting his tie fall back down in front of him. He's the only guy I know who changes into his designer suit as soon as he's done surfing so he can head into the office.

"I have the kid tomorrow."

He shrugs. "Give him your phone and he'll be quiet. I've seen my clients do it a million times."

I nod, turning around to leave the restaurant.

For some reason, Payne doesn't seem like a kid who can be distracted by a phone, but I pray that Jagger's right.

———

THE NEXT DAY at seven in the morning I knock on Layla's front door so that I can start my first shift as The Manny. I would've thought I'd be more nervous than I am, but I figure he's just a kid. How hard can watching a kid who can talk, walk and feed himself be, really?

The door swings open and Layla stands there, her hair askew, still in what looks to be her pajamas with some type of crusted food implanted right between her tits. Her eyes are wide and she's panting hard as if she just finished running the New York marathon.

"Vance. Hi. Come in." She waves me in, clearly in a hurry.

Shit. Did the paps follow me?

I step inside and close the door behind me since she's already walking away.

"I have a huge favor to ask you and I wouldn't ask unless I was desperate. Which I am," she says.

"The last time you asked me for a favor I became a full

time caregiver for your son. What is it this time?" I'm only half-kidding but I keep my voice light.

"I slept past my alarm and for once in my life the kids didn't actually wake me up. I'm going to be late for my call time if I don't leave in the next three minutes. Is there any chance that you could get Via dressed and drop her off at daycare? I just finished feeding her breakfast."

She doesn't wait for me to answer before she's halfway through the archway.

I don't know shit about babies and though I'd normally tell her not a chance in hell, how can I say no. She's clearly in a jam and it's easy to garner a bad reputation in this town when you're late and cost the production team time and money.

Stamp sucker on my forehead. "Sure. Just text me the address for the daycare," I say.

The relief and gratitude etched on Layla's face confirms I made the right decision and I'm happy that I'm able to help her out. "You're a life saver." She reaches forward and squeezes both of my hands. "I already laid Via's clothes for the day out. You just have to take that bag by the door." She points to the area behind me, "and the car seats are in the garage. You can google the instructions for installing them if you run into a problem, but you're a smart guy, so I doubt you will." She winks. As though she doesn't already have me by the balls and needs to compliment me.

I nod, trying to commit all the instructions to memory. My morning routine usually involves me showering, dressing and grabbing a coffee. "Fair enough. You go get ready and I'll handle things down here.

She gives me a big smile then spins on her heel and races toward the stairs.

I spend the next few minutes playing with Payne while Via blabbers contentedly in her high chair and plays with the small container Layla must have had her breakfast in. Less than five minutes later Layla races down the stairs, says a quick goodbye to the kids, and then tosses a 'call me if you need me' out behind her.

I clap my hands together. "Okay guys, what do you say we head upstairs to get you both dressed?"

Payne screams and runs up the stairs while I figure out how to get Via out of her high chair. A minute later and I'm smiling to myself at the small victory as we walk across the kitchen. That's when it hits me—a scent so putrid it should be used as a form of warfare.

"Oh God." I plug my nose. "What did you eat?"

As soon as the words leave my mouth it dawns on me that there's only one person in this house who can change her diaper—me. From the smell of this little girl, it's going to be one for the record books.

I find Payne upstairs standing in the hallway waiting for me.

"Can you show me which one is your sister's room?" I ask him.

"Ya." He skips through a door on his right and I follow him into a room with lavender painted walls, white furniture and a pale grey rocking chair. "Eww, Via!" He stops, plugs his nose. Tell me about it kid. "You have to change her diaper." He runs over, grabs a diaper and throws it at me.

"Yeah, I get it." I lie Via down on the floor.

"Not there." Payne points up to the table where he got the diaper. "There."

Oh yeah, makes sense. I pick up Via and hold her face forward away from my new shirt. She giggles and squirms. My eyes fixate on her back because common sense tells me the shit has to go somewhere.

I place Via down on the cushioned table. She immediately

tries to roll over so I place my hand in the middle of her chest so that she stays put.

Another waft of what's in her diaper makes its way to my nose. I hold my breath and press my lips together. "Is my script really this important?" I mumble.

"Payne, can you go get your clothes on?"

"Can I pick my own shirt?" he asks.

"Sure buddy, wear whatever you want."

"Yay!" He races from the room and drawers are slamming seconds later.

Via is gazing up at me with her big blue eyes and smile on her face. "I bet you're feeling lighter now."

She giggles as if she can understand what I'm saying and I suppress a smile. Time to get serious. Get in and get out. *Successful scriptwriter. Sundance. Sony.* I repeat the reasons I'm in this position over and over again.

Once I've pumped myself up enough, I unzip her pajamas and lift her legs out of the feet holders, then her arms. Clean stomach, although she's packing a nice size bulge in her diaper. Then I realize, there's shit on the pajamas and I drop them in the laundry basket. I tear off one side of the diaper and then the other, and inhale one last breath before I pull the diaper down. "Holy shit!" How can a little girl's poop be as big as Leo's dog, Cooper's shit?

Bile races up my throat and I physically swallow back the vomit, leaving a path of fire back down. I press my hand to my mouth and turn my head to take a few fresh air deep breaths.

"What am I supposed to do now?"

I am in way over my head. Changing my first diaper is one thing. Changing my first diaper full of shit and dealing with a biological disaster is another entirely.

With my free hand, I pull my phone out from my back pocket, ready to call Layla but the last thing she needs to realize is her new scriptwriter can't even change a diaper. Luckily, there's one other woman in my life who happened to be the go-to babysitter in Climax Cove— my sister Charlie. Besides she's pregnant. She's probably been practicing with dolls so she's prepared when the day comes.

I thumb through my contacts and press on her name. I hit the speaker button and set my phone down on the dresser beside the bin holding the clean diapers.

"Vance?" she answers on the second ring.

"Hey. I need your help."

"Hello to you too, Vance. How is life in LA? Oh, I'm fine. Why yes, the pregnancy is going great," she says in a sweet voice. "But then you'd know that if you answered my texts!" she says much angrier.

"Sorry I've been busy. Listen. Hypothetically speaking let's say you had a baby on a table and she took a giant shit and it ended up all the way up her back...what's the first thing you would do?" I ask.

"Hypothetically speaking? Cut the shit, what's going on?" she counters.

"I see that loving motherly side hasn't surfaced yet."

"That comment isn't going to win you any points," she says. "Garrett not now." She giggles. "I'm on the phone with my brother." Another giggle.

My stomach rolls. As if this situation isn't bad enough, I now have to listen to one of my best friends seduce my sister. He already got her pregnant what more does he want? Kill me now.

"Would you guys stop that? I'm serious. I need help." Panic is laced through my every word.

"Okay, okay. I'm getting out of bed," she says.

"That is a visual I don't need."

"Beggars can't be choosers, Vance. Do you want my help with your hypothetical situation?"

I blow out a breath. "Yes, please."

"There's the son mom raised. Now, is she still in her clothes?" she asks.

"No. What next?" I ask, eager for this to be over.

"Where did you put it?"

"In the laundry basket. Is that bad?" I ask.

She laughs. "It's not bad but everything in there will have to be washed as soon as you're done there."

"Sure, whatever. So what do I do next?"

"Are there any diaper wipes around you?"

I search the area and spot a plastic tub labeled diaper wipes. "Got them."

"Okay, this isn't going to be fun brother, but there's no way around it. You're going to have to take her diaper off and when you do try to roll it up and use the tabs on the side to keep the poop inside."

"How the hell am I supposed to do that when this kid keeps trying to roll off the table?"

"You just are."

"I wouldn't go writing a how to book any time soon," I grind out, using my free hand to pop open the lid and pull a few wipes out.

"Watch it, I'm not against hanging up."

"Sorry," I sigh. "It's just this is ..."

"Let's get this over with and then you can tell me what kind of woman has you changing her baby's diapers. Now, there's probably a Diaper Genie somewhere close. Put the diaper in that."

"Charlie, if there was a diaper genie anywhere around here you can bet your ass I wouldn't be doing this."

My sister's laugh echoes through the phone speaker and Via follows suit, giggling on her own and sucking on a few of her fingers.

"A Diaper Genie is what you put dirty diapers in so they don't stink up the whole house, Vance. It's white and plastic."

I lean over to look at the ground on either side of the change table. "I see it," I say, happy for the small victory.

"All right, do what you need to and tell me when you're done. I'll wait on the line."

My stomach lurches and I gag before I get myself under control. Somehow I manage to half roll the diaper but I'm not sure it makes much of a difference. Shit is everywhere I look.

I take the scrunched up diaper and step on the foot pedal of the Diaper Genie and push the damn thing down until it disappears.

I'm bringing my hand back up to grab a wet wipe when I see the brown smear along the side of my index finger.

"Oh fuck. No way!"

"Vance what's wrong?" Charlie asks.

"There's shit on my finger. There is actual shit on my finger!" I cringe. This was way more than I bargained for.

"Tell that pussy to man up," Garrett yells in the background. "Does he have any idea how many shitty diapers of Syd's I changed?"

"Whatever man, you've never seen anything like this," I yell back on the off chance he can hear me.

I use my elbow to hold Via in place and take the diaper wipe in my other hand, furiously scrubbing at the spot. Once it's gone I take another one and do the same just to be sure. It's not until I'm finished that I realize that Charlie is laughing at me.

"What the hell are you laughing at?" I ask.

"You. A little poop isn't going to kill you, Vance." She starts laughing again.

"Excuse me but have you not heard of e-coli before?" I rip

a few more wet wipes from the container. "Let's get this over with. What now?"

"Take both her ankles in one hand and raise them to lift her butt . Then use the diaper wipes to clean her up. If she's chubby make sure you get in all the folds. Front to back."

"Front to back?"

"Don't pretend you don't know your way around a pussy, Vance. Place the wipe in the front and go back. You don't want to get any poop in her hooha."

I shudder, but not wanting to prolong this I get to work. After a few swipes I realize I have a problem. "There's poop on the change pad."

"That's okay. See if you can get her mostly cleaned up, then remove it and put it in the laundry and wipe the plastic part of the change pad down."

A few minutes later, mission accomplished Via lays on the change table in a clean diaper, pulling her foot up to her mouth. I release a relieved breath.

"Thanks, Sis. I owe you one."

"Yes, you do. I'll take payment in the form of you telling me what the hell you've gotten yourself into."

I roll my eyes. "Sure thing. But right now I have to go check to make sure a four-year-old little boy isn't cooking meth or something in his bedroom. It's too quiet in there."

She laughs. "Vance, you better call me later. I'm sure you'd rather that then me and Garrett surprising you in LA, right?"

"Hell yes. I'll call you tonight. Promise."

I hang up and slide the phone into my back pocket and then pick up Via. "What do you say we go check on your brother then I'll go buy you a new outfit to replace that one?"

She squeals and smacks the top of my head with her palm.

I'll take that as a yes.

———

NINE AM, after a full hour of trying to properly install both car seats in my truck, I've dropped Via off at daycare and I'm finally on our way over to Jagger's office. I swear you need to be a NASA scientist to install those damn things. I hadn't realized that I needed an engineering degree for this manny job.

"Remember, we're really quiet when we're in here," I remind Payne as we enter the empty elevator.

He pinches his lips together and nods his head.

What is Layla complaining about? So far Payne seems to be able to take instruction well.

"Great, buddy. It won't be long." I ruffle his hair, the blond strands such a contrast from his mom's, yet so similar to what his dad is known for.

The elevator dings and I file out, walking toward Jagger's office. A small hand slides into mine.

Shit, I should be holding his hand. I tighten my grip and smile down at him.

*Okay, I got this.*

"Hey, Victoria."

Her gaze falls to the little guy next to me and then back to me, her eyes full of questions. "Who's your friend?" She leans forward on her desk and smiles at Payne.

"This is Payne." I pause. "Payne, this is Victoria."

"Hello, Payne." She waves, her toothy smile trying to put him at ease.

The little guy slinks closer to my body, his gaze shifting around everywhere.

"Well, he's waiting for you." She rolls back in her chair and watches us walk by her desk and into Jagger's office.

Jagger starts in on me as soon as I close the door behind us. "Hey. Glad you're here early. We have ten minutes to prepare you. What are you wearing?" He looks me up and down. I follow his vision to my t-shirt and jeans.

"It's a conference call," I argue.

"A *video* conference call." He blows out a breath, straightens his tie and looks down at Payne. "Hey, buddy, you must be Payne."

Again, the kid clings harder to my hand and uses me as a shield.

"He's not up for talking this morning."

Jagger's eyes dart from him to me and back again, then he shakes his head.

I walk over to the couch. "Can you stay here while I'm on this call?" I ask Payne.

He nods.

"Here's my phone, there are five games for you to play." I silence it and hand it over to him.

He gives me a huge smile and starts playing immediately.

"Told you," Jagger brags and I sit down at the table, realizing there's already a camera set up on the opposite end. "I talked to Hannah this morning. We're all set. She couldn't be more thrilled to hear that Layla accepted."

Guess I underestimated Jagger. He may actually understand kids. I downloaded five games. Ten dollars is a small price to pay for me to have a conference call in silence. He isn't even antsy when Victoria sneaks in to tell him she has something cool to show him—he just follows her out, barely taking his eyes off the screen.

A half hour later Jagger is clicking out of the conference call and I'm breathing a sigh of relief. Hannah seems like a decent woman and she's really enthusiastic over the project. Seems we're heading in the right direction.

"We're set, man," Jagger says and pushes away from the boardroom table and walks over to his desk. "All the paperwork should be done tonight. Now, you need to find the rest of your team. I can set up some interviews for you if you need me to." Jagger has faults, but at his job, he is a lean, mean, efficient machine. Crossing T's and dotting I's are the least of what he does to be perfect in his job.

I run my hands down my pants. "I'm nervous."

"Why? This is what you've always wanted."

I wonder if fear is even a word in Jagger's dictionary.

"Yeah, I want it, but fuck." I push my hand through my hair. "I'm not good with failure."

He waves me off. "You're not going to fail. This is a killer script. Do you really think I'd attach my name to a shitty project?" His egotistical smirk crosses his lips and I can't help but smile. "Calm down and enjoy the ride, but I do want to warn you of one thing." He glances out the window of his office, and then sets his determined gaze back on me. "Do *not* get involved with Layla Andrews."

I relax back in my seat, resting my ankle on my knee. "Obviously, why would I?"

He points at me. "That look on your face when her name comes up in conversation. You had it yesterday and you have it today."

"There's no look." I chuckle from the sheer ridiculousness of this conversation.

"Yes, there is. You'd have to be fucking blind not to see it. You had that same look with Gwen Sinclair last year. Remember how that turned out?" He raises his perfectly manscaped eyebrows. Someone needs to tell him that real men don't need to get buffed and waxed at a salon, even if they bang the aesthetician on occasion.

"Why do you have to bring that shit up?"

"Because it's the point to me telling you what to do. Hands off the actresses."

"I wasn't the fucking scriptwriter, not to mention you know there's a helluva lot more to that story."

He nods, sporting those sympathetic eyes I fled from months prior. "I know that. Why do you think I don't fuck them? They're always drama." He pauses briefly. "You just need to remember that it never does anyone any good to fuck where you eat."

"The waitress at the taco place?" I shoot him a look suggesting he's full of it.

"Okay, okay. Figuratively, not literally. Now, I have emails to respond to, so go be a babysitter and don't let the little mommy seduce you." He straightens in his chair, turning in the direction of his computer.

"Well then, don't let me hold you up." I stand and walk over to the door.

"Vance."

I stop at the door, my hand on the knob.

"Just remember what I said. This is your chance, let's not blow it with a scandal."

I don't turn around. Instead, I nod and open the door to escape the lecture of a man who is a master at his job, but needs to take the agent hat off and put his friend hat back on.

Closing the door behind me, I find Payne spinning in Victoria's office chair, the arms hitting her desk on every turn.

"Where's Victoria?" I ask.

"Getting me lunch." He spins again and I grab her mug of water before it spills over.

"She left you?" I grab my phone off the desk and place my hand on the chair to stop it from spinning.

"She's getting me something to eat."

"I fed you on the way over." I lean my butt against the desk and cross my arms over my chest.

"Cheerios. Via eats Cheerios." He rolls his eyes and then glances toward the garbage.

Standing up, I see the bag sitting in the trash. "Fine, but when she gets back, we're leaving."

I hear Victoria's heels click behind me. "Hey, you're done already?" she asks.

I stand up. "You're lucky your desk is still in one piece."

"I was only gone for five minutes. Payne promised he'd stay seated." She smiles at him and he spins in her chair again, hitting the desk so that her bottle of water falls, a puddle forming all over her desk.

"Shit!" I say, hurriedly picking up the bottle.

Payne stands up when the water falls on his legs and stares at his pants. Victoria drops the bag of food and reaches over with some napkins, soaking up the liquid right away. She's calm and doesn't seem at all pissed that half her papers are soaked.

"I can reprint them," she tells Payne. "It's just a mistake, right?" She smiles at him and the look of fear on Payne's face disintegrates.

"Do you have kids?" I ask her after she's handed Payne a small hamburger and fries.

She glances back to Jagger's office and then to me. "Yeah. I'm a single mom," she says in a quiet voice.

"My mom too," Payne chirps in.

A soft smile forms on her lips. "She must be pretty cool then."

Payne chomps down on his fries, his legs swinging under the chair.

"Are you keeping it a secret?" I ask.

Again, she glances at Jagger's door like she's afraid he'll overhear us. "You know Jagger, rumor is that he doesn't like his employees to have kids."

I wave her off. "That's absurd. He wouldn't care."

She shrugs and her phone pages, Jagger's voice not waiting for her to answer.

"Tell my best friend and the kid to get lost. You have work to do."

Before I can even offer a smartass comment back the line clicks off.

She raises both eyebrows and sits down at her desk, trying to clean up Payne's mess.

Jagger's words echo in my mind as we step into the elevator and I send a little prayer up that I'm not well on my way to creating my own mess that has to be cleaned up.

**9**

**Layla**

I walk into my house with Via on my hip at the end of a long day to the sound of Linkin Park blaring over the stereo. Seems like Payne's going to learn those last few swear words he doesn't already know.

Via wiggles in my arms and I place her down on the ground, where she immediately runs off toward the noise coming from the kitchen and living area.

"Invaders!" Payne screams and he runs past me to duck behind the couch, Via following close behind.

Two seconds later, Vance runs in wearing protective eyewear and a vest, with a Nerf gun in his hand.

"Me! Me!" Via runs out from behind the couch, holding her hands out for his gun.

He bends down to her and she grabs the glasses from his face and throws them on the floor. Payne comes from behind the couch and Vance's vest lights up.

"Gotcha," Payne shouts.

"You planned that distraction. I call foul." Vance laughs as Via points the Nerf gun at him and somehow figures out how to fire off a dart.

Exaggerating an injury, Vance falls to the ground and Via jumps on top of him, laughing the way only a small child can —as if nothing in the world has ever been funnier than this moment.

"Whoa. I thought your brother was bad." He picks her up with both hands under her arms and sets her to his side.

"Well, I think Via and I had a boring day compared to yours," I say with a smile.

His cheeks turn the lightest shade of pink and he brushes off his jeans. Note to self—call cleaning lady. Also note to self —Vance is completely adorable when he's embarrassed. "I wasn't expecting you so early."

"I'd hoped to let you off the hook earlier." I pick up Via because she might be all fun and games right now, but if she doesn't eat soon we'll be facing off with someone who's more psychotic than Kim Jong-un.

"Hey, we made a deal. Don't go light on me." He makes his way over to the stereo, turning the music off, and then comes to lean on the archway into the kitchen. His arms are crossed, the t-shirt he's wearing tight around his biceps, and with the Nerf vest on and the goofy smile plastered on his face he's somehow more attractive, not less. How is that even possible?

"Come on, Vance." Payne pulls on the hem of Vance's t-shirt. "Again. Let's play."

Vance looks down at Payne. "Let me catch your mom up."

"Payne, I'm going to start dinner. Go clean up the toys."

Payne rolls his eyes and Vance moves to take off his vest, which results in his shirt rising and me discovering he has a teasing patch of happy trail that disappears down past the waistband of his jeans.

A throat-clearing distracts me as I'm trying to strap Via into her high chair. My eyes snap up and Vance's smirk is set in place, as is the blazing heat in his eyes, heat I need doused.

*I cannot fall for the scriptwriter.*

"I ordered pizza," Vance says, letting the moment pass.

He might as well have said that he'd like me laid out on the counter spread-eagle for him because nothing has made me happier in this moment than knowing I don't have to cook dinner.

"Oh, you didn't have to do that."

*Thank you, thank you, thank you.*

"I know filming can go late," Vance says.

Via smacks my hand and my head turns in her direction. "Yum, yum."

"Yeah, well, when your role is as small as mine is, that's not as much of a problem." I make my way to the cabinet, grabbing a box of crackers. I place a few on the tray and grab her sippy cup out of the fridge. That should hold her off until the pizza comes, so I sit down in a kitchen chair, propping my feet up on the vacant seat across from me.

"Hard day?" Vance asks and straddles the chair, picking up my feet and placing them between his open legs. His two hands mould one of my feet, hitting all the right spots.

"Probably not as hard as yours." I don't pull away even though I shouldn't be allowing this to happen, but damn, his hands are magic.

"Payne isn't bad. Just energetic. I don't think I need to work out while I'm watching him." He smiles at me and then concentrates back on my feet.

"Thank you."

He nods, switching feet. "I don't want to start trouble or anything, but I thought you said Carver was filming?" His attention focuses in on me to judge my reaction.

"He is." As soon as the words leave my mouth I know I'm obviously in the dark about something. Something that's probably splashed all over *TMZ*.

"He's not."

I close my eyes and inhale a deep breath. "Just tell me."

"He was spotted at LAX this morning with Gwen Sinclair." The flirtatious eyes and smirk he's been giving me all night are gone. Now it's the 'I'm sorry I'm the one who had to tell you' look.

"I'm not surprised. The man never makes seeing his kids a priority. Of course, he'd pick the one actress I hate in this industry." I pull my feet from Vance's hands and walk over to the fridge, grabbing the bottle of wine.

"You hate Gwen?" he asks, following me to stand across from me, leaning against my counter.

"It's stupid, but she got a part over me and I've always thought she did something sleazy to get it. I know I nailed that audition and I was told it was as good as mine, but then I got a call a few days later that they'd decided to go another direction." I pour myself a hefty glass.

I shouldn't have said anything to Vance, I don't want him to think I'm difficult. What kind of actress holds it against another that she got the part? It's just... something never sat right with me about how everything went down. Regardless, I shouldn't hold her reputation of being everyone's plaything against her. Who knows if it's true.

He nods, not looking at me but down at the floor now. "Do you have any beer?"

"I have a few in the fridge for when my dad visits. Help yourself."

The urge to pull out my phone and check out *TMZ* to see if they have the whole story on Carver is strong, but I resist —for now.

I lower my voice so Via or Payne can't hear me. "You know the thing is, I don't give a shit who he fucks—it's the kids. He told me he would still be out of town. I mean, can't he see his children at all? Not even to take them to get an ice cream cone or something?" I down a large slug of my wine just as the doorbell rings.

"I'll get that." Vance walks out of the room.

Should I have kept my mouth shut? He's taking a chance on casting me in a leading role, I coerced him into being my manny, and now I want him to sign up as my therapist too?

*God, get a grip, Layla.*

Vance walks back in a minute later with a large pizza in his hand.

"Let me pay you." I move for my bag, but he grabs a hold of my wrist.

"I got it."

Payne runs in the room, free of all his Nerf stuff, and Vance raises his hand for a high-five. "Great job cleaning up, buddy. I had a fun day." Payne smacks his hand and Vance looks over to me. "Same time tomorrow?"

I nod.

"Are you not staying for pizza?" Payne's voice sounds like it does when his father leaves.

Could they really have connected that fast?

"Tomorrow, I'm thinking..." Vance puts his finger to his lips. "Trampoline park?"

"Yay!" Payne jumps around with his arms in the air.

While Payne celebrates my gaze finds Vance and we share a look. I have no idea what it is but it's weighted with emotion. Almost like he's apologizing, which is absurd. It's not his fault my ex can't take time away from his latest conquest to see his own kids.

"See you, Via," Vance says with a small wave.

She smiles over her mouthful of crackers and I follow Vance out of the kitchen.

"Thank you again. Payne had a good time, I can tell."

He stops at the front door. "I had fun. You have a great kid."

I'm not sure he means it, but Payne so rarely receives compliments that I'm glad someone sees the diamond inside of him.

"I'll see you tomorrow," I say, trying not to let the note of sadness I'm feeling at his departure creep into my voice.

"See you."

He turns and speeds down my walkway, no backward glances or lingering looks, which shouldn't surprise me. I'm sure like everyone else he has a life he wants to get back to.

With a small smile I head back into the kitchen, to the two most important things in my own life, telling myself that one day I'll find someone who shares that sentiment, but not really believing it to be true.

**10**

## Layla

On day two of Manny Vance, I walk into the house with the baby and it's a completely different scene than the night prior. The first thing I notice is that they're not running around. Instead, Vance is sprawled out on the couch with his feet on my coffee table and Payne is cuddled under his arm fast asleep.

Vance smiles that panty-melting grin he seems to have been born with. As soon as we enter the room Via screams and wiggles out of my hold, running over to Vance and hitting him on the leg.

Vance tries to get up, but it's clear from the way he's trying to extricate himself that he's afraid he'll wake Payne, so I rush over, pick up Payne and hold him to my chest.

"He does this sometimes when he's going through a growth spurt. Experience has shown me that it's better to let him sleep through the night and double up on breakfast otherwise he can be a bear. I'll be right back," I whisper, casting a glance Via's way. "Can you keep an eye on her for a sec?"

"I can take him," he offers, standing up with his hands out.

"That's okay. I've got it."

Fear flashes across his face and I stifle a laugh so as not to wake up Payne. Apparently, Vance is okay with four-year-olds but not kids under two.

Tiptoeing upstairs, I lay Payne on his bed, slowly strip him of his jeans and tuck him in. I can't help but stare at him while he's sleeping. I swear until I had kids I didn't even know this was an urge I'd ever have. He has his dad's prominent nose and perfect lips and I know that one day he'll be breaking hearts like him, but I know it's going to be my job to teach Payne to respect women and the institution of marriage. I sit down on the edge of the bed and brush the blond strands from his eyes, recalling last night's dinner and how he had a zillion stories about Vance and how cool he is. I was worried at first, but this manny idea has turned out to be great for him.

When I reach the bottom of the stairs, Via's giggle echoes into the foyer.

*What could they be doing?*

I round the corner finding Via pressing a button on the ball machine that's been jammed for the past two months. I kept meaning to buy another one because she had loved it so much, but life and time haven't really been on my side.

"You fixed it?" I ask, making my way through the room, picking up the Legos, the Ninja Turtles, and every other mismatched toy strewn on the floor.

"Yeah," he answers, leaning back on the couch with his legs stretched out, snatching balls from the machine right after they pop out, making Via laugh even more.

"You hungry, Via?" I ask, dropping all the toys into the one mass bin they're stored in. Long gone are my anal days when I'd spend an hour arranging each category of toy back into organized bins. Life no longer allows me such luxuries.

"Yum," she says.

Unlike last night Vance doesn't seem in a rush to get out of here, which, if I'm honest, secretly pleases me.

"Would you like to stay for dinner?" I ask him, and before you get all judgy, know that I'm doing it because he's been so great the last two days and dinner is the least I can do.

"You cook?" His right eyebrow quirks up.

"I thought you would have realized by now that I'm not some spoiled starlet." I wink and then spin on my heel and head into the kitchen, not waiting for an answer.

My head is in the fridge by the time I hear Via's light footsteps enter the room. When I glance over I see that Vance is right behind her.

"Honestly?" He thinks he's so suave, his hip resting on the island in the kitchen, his arms crossed and that damn smirk on display.

I take the chicken I had in the fridge and place it on the counter then turn to face him, waiting for him to continue.

"I thought you were a prima donna, making me come to the trailer to present the script when a courier could have sent it over."

I unwrap the butcher paper, move over to the cabinet, and grab a knife and cutting board. "I apologize for that. I'd gotten off the phone with Carver minutes before and it put me in a bad mood. In my head I was thinking if they want me so bad, show me." I shook my head, staring down at the raw chicken. "I'm sorry."

"You should be happy I don't go off first impressions." He chuckles, and I remember our conversation from Yolk Me. He comes over and takes the knife from my hands. "I got this. What are we making?"

"Stir-fry."

He licks his lips. "Yum."

"Yum," Via echoes from where she's playing on the floor with one of her toys.

Vance glances her way and then laughs at her, his eyes lighting in amusement.

It's like overload for my brain. Do I focus on how hot it looked when he licked his lips or think about how adorable it was when he laughed at my daughter? A girl can only take so much. At least one who's been celibate as long as I have.

Not noticing my reaction, he takes one of the chicken breasts and places it on the cutting board.

"You know how to cook?" I ask him, raising my eyebrows and mimicking his earlier question.

"Nah, but I do know my way around a good set of breasts. Have faith."

I laugh at his bad joke and as I back away, I try my damnedest not to think about what he could probably do with my breasts if I let him.

———

An hour later, we're at the table finishing up dinner while Via's spreads what's left of hers all over the tray of her high chair.

"Thanks for dinner," Vance says, wiping his mouth with a napkin.

"You can hardly thank me when you did half the work."

Vance chopped the chicken and the vegetables. All I did was make the rice and mix the sauce.

"I never cook for myself. I came back from my hometown a few weeks ago and I haven't had a home-cooked meal since. This was great." He pushes his empty plate away from him and leans back in his chair.

"Where are you from?" I ask, curious to know more.

"Up in Oregon. Small town."

I nod. "Small towns are nice. I grew up in one, too." The memory of my own small-town upbringing in Kentucky flashes through my mind.

"They can be. I bet when you cross the county line you get a police escort." He smiles.

A small laugh huffs out of me. "Yeah, but I'm also the first one they call when the town needs money."

No joke. And I want to help my town, they helped me become who I am, but it's hard to hand a check over to the girl who bullied you throughout grade school.

"Your parents still there?" he asks. I'm guessing his are still in his home town. Otherwise why would he return? I can't remember the last time I went home.

"No. They've moved on up. Malibu now."

I spare him the tragic child star tale about how all the money they have was money I earned. Not that I begrudge taking care of my parents, but when you're fourteen and the only breadwinner in a family there's an unbelievable amount of pressure to succeed. Maybe that's why I've been okay since Carver left. I'm used to being the one who has to step up and take care of everybody else's needs, leaving my own on the backburner.

"That's pretty close. Must be nice for the kids."

I shrug, pushing my plate away and taking in the state of Via's high chair tray. "Yeah, they watch the kids when they aren't traveling."

I walk over to the sink because Via's about to have rice as a headpiece if I don't wipe her down soon.

On my way back to the table, I find Vance's gaze on me. He has a way of making me feel wanton with just one look. As though he's itching to have his hands on me, and is struggling to control himself. I wish I didn't like it so much.

Pulling my own gaze away from him, I concentrate on

cleaning Via up. When I pick her up from the high chair, she rests her head on my shoulder.

"Give me five?" I ask.

He stands up, collecting his dish and mine. "I think I can keep myself busy." His smirk is on display as he walks toward the sink.

"Please don't clean. I'll get to it—"

"When?" His eyebrows quirk up.

"I manage." Via goes limp in my arms. Daycare must have been a busy place today.

"Go put your daughter to bed, Layla." With his back turned to me, he starts moving the dishes from the stove over to the sink and I hear the faucet turn on before I reach the bottom of the stairs.

Via should have a bath. I should rock her to sleep like I usually do, but she's out like she's the mother of two young kids, so I change her diaper and clothes and place her into her crib, where she settles again after a few moments.

Moving on to Payne's room, I see that he's moved from the bed to the floor.

I slide my hands underneath him in an effort to get him back into his bed. "Oh, you're so big now," I whisper to myself and place him on the mattress, pulling the covers up over him.

The picture of him and Carver next to the bed pulls me in to remembering what I thought my life would be like. We were going to beat the odds. We'd win the Hollywood lottery and be the ones to enjoy successful careers *and* a successful marriage. Now I'd just be happy if the kids saw more of him in person than they do in that ridiculous sour cream commercial he's in.

I mean, come on—the man doesn't even eat anything white. I'm not lying. Nope. Sour cream, mayonnaise, yogurt. He won't touch anything dairy that's white. Maybe that revelation should've been my first inkling that something was off.

I sigh and rise up off the bed, leaving Payne's room and making a quick stop in my own before I head back downstairs. I give myself the once-over in my mirror, taking in my tired eyes and the grey underneath. After a quick dab of face powder, I pinch my cheeks to bring out their natural rosiness, readjust my breasts in my bra so they're sitting pretty and decide I'm as ready as I'll ever be. For what, I can't be sure.

Do I want Vance? Hell, yes. But I'm smart enough to know I shouldn't. But no one's ever been hurt by basking in the feeling of someone else's eyes smoldering when they look at you, right? Not to mention, I'm a single mother and a working actress with no real social life unless it's something my PR people tell me to go to. Sue me if it feels nice to be wanted after having a husband who couldn't stop wanting everyone else.

The dishwasher is loaded and Vance is cleaning Via's high chair tray when I reach downstairs.

"You have any idea how long it took me to figure out how to unlatch this?" He eyes the soapy tray he's scouring with a sponge.

I chuckle. "I know, they should call it adult-proofing. When Payne was younger, I had this toilet seat lock..." I shake my head—I should not be telling this story.

"Yeah?" he says, looking over his shoulder at me, a laugh ready behind his smile.

"Never mind."

He turns around, drying his hands on the dishtowel. "No, no, tell me."

I prop myself up on the counter, tucking my hands under my thighs. "We were away at a hotel and I woke up in the middle of the night. Long story short, I ended up with my ass in the sink."

He buckles over in laughter. "Shower wasn't a better option?"

I pick up the hot pad next to me and throw it at him. "It was two in the morning. My brain wasn't functioning."

His jeans mould to his ass when he bends over to pick up the hot pad and I don't bother pretending not to stare. He eyes the drawer under my legs where the hot pad belongs. I should jump off the counter, take the hot pad from his hands and put it back in the drawer.

I don't.

It's like a slow-motion montage in a movie. He saunters over, one hand landing on the inside of my knee, easing it apart while his other hand opens the drawer. The hot pad drops and he shuts the drawer as I swallow hard, his eyes never leaving mine. His other hand pushes my other leg to the side and my breaths become shallow.

My girly parts are on high alert, begging me to slide forward on the counter, let his hands skim the outside of my legs and mould to my ass.

One kiss won't hurt anyone. I could just get it out of my system and move on. There's nothing wrong with that.

"Layla." My name sounds like a soft plea from his lips.

"Yes?" I press my lips together and his gaze drops, taking in the motion.

I realize too late that his hands have moved to the outside of my thighs. He pulls me forward and my hands fall to his shoulders.

"Just one taste," he says, one hand snaking its way up my neck until he tilts my head and his lips crash down onto mine.

Our kiss is sweet and raw and still it leaves me starving for more. It all mixes together into a cocktail that has be drunk off of Vance Rose. Our tongues glide, our lips meld, and the kiss is like the moment on the Fourth of July when the first firework blasts through the night sky while the crowd oohs and awws, eager for what's to come. I know by the way he's devouring me that our kiss is merely the promise of what Vance can do to my body.

Our hands become frantic, clawing and grasping and taking whatever we can. He lifts me from the counter and my back smacks against the wall. I instinctively wrap my legs around his waist, the rigid length of him grinding against my center. Our tongues delve deeper, our mouths explore even more while my hands twirl the light brown hair at the base of his neck.

"Mommy?"

"Shit," Vance murmurs, steps away from me, and my feet barely land on the floor in time to catch myself.

Vance turns around, opening the fridge door to hide his upper half inside.

"Payne." I try to catch my breath. "What's wrong, baby?"

"I'm hungry."

"Okay, let's get you fed now that you're up."

I guide him over to the kitchen table and upon my return to the kitchen cabinets Vance finally shuts the fridge door. I hope I don't look as dishevelled as him.

"I better get going. See you two tomorrow." He smiles, one that doesn't quite reach his eyes.

Payne's already half passed out on the table, but manages to give Vance a high-five on his way out.

"I'll be right back," I say to Payne, following Vance out. "You don't have to leave."

*How pathetic do I sound?*

Vance turns around, putting his black leather coat on. "Yeah, I do." There's a finality to his voice and I realize that he thinks the kiss was a mistake. Knowing he's right does nothing to ease the sting.

"Thank you for today and for cleaning up. I have an interview set up for a nanny tomorrow after work."

Vance nods. "Thanks again for dinner, Layla." A small spark travels through my body and zings me right in the heart when he says my name.

"You're welcome."

He opens the door and I hold it open for him to leave. He stops on the stoop outside and turns around, his eyes roaming up and down my body, pausing for a moment on my lips before he raises his gaze to my eyes.

"Oh, I forgot," he says.

To kiss me goodnight?

"Yeah?" My breasts push out and his gaze dips but recovers too fast for my liking.

"I picked up your dry cleaning. It's in the front hallway." He winks.

"You didn't have to do that, but thanks." My shoulders falter and I have to remember he's many roles in my life. He's my new scriptwriter, my kid's manny, but he's not my conquest. He's not someone I can sleep with. No matter how much I want him and how sweet and thoughtful he seems.

He steps back up the steps, his hand moulding to my cheek. "You're an amazing woman. You have your hands full and I noticed the slip on the counter." He shrugs. "I'm glad I could take one thing off your list."

I lick my lips, ready for another kiss, but his hand falls from my cheek and he steps back.

"Good night," he mumbles and disappears down the walkway.

I shut the door, my hand still clutched around the door handle while I gather myself.

"Mommy," Payne says from behind me and I startle.

"Don't scare Mommy." I lock the door, and lead Payne back to the kitchen.

"How come Vance was licking your neck?" he asks.

*Shit.*

"I'd spilled something on myself and we ran out of napkins." Not my best excuse, but this is uncharted territory for me. Since Payne's half asleep he takes me at my word.

I look around at the clean kitchen, think of the dry-cleaning hanging in the hall closet and how Vance will be back tomorrow to watch Payne. It may only be temporary, but it's a relief to have someone else to rely on and not have everything resting on my shoulders alone.

I'll carry the load alone if I must, but I'm beginning to understand that it's so much sweeter when there's someone there sharing the weight of it all.

## 11

## Vance

"**I**'m worried." Leo glances away from the Golden Retriever he's shampooing in his doggie spa to where Payne is hanging out by the puppy corral.

"What?" I pop a chip into my mouth as I sit on the counter watching him.

"The kid looks at you like you're Spider-Man. You're playing with fire. He's attached after only three days."

"Nah, Payne loves Ninja Turtles. He's on the fence with Spider-Man." I pop another chip into my mouth.

Leo shoots me his annoyed look. What can I say? I know what he's saying, but I can't be expected to control how awesome I am.

"You know what I mean." He hoses off the big dog, the water spraying back onto his shirt, causing it to cling to his chest.

"Do you have that window so women can ogle you?" I look through the cut-out in the wall at the four women sipping their Starbucks and admiring the scene unfolding in front of them.

"No." He glances at them, too, then back to the dog. "I do it so the owners can see what we're doing."

"Uh-huh, whatever. Clearly those women haven't heard the rumors." I chuckle and Leo shakes his head.

Besides his doggie spa Leo creates and sells dog clothes on some website that starts with an 'E'. When people find that out they make their own assumptions and Leo never bothers to refute them. Apparently, a single heterosexual man can't be good at designing and sewing dog clothes.

"They can assume all they want. I don't lie." Leo shoots me a look of warning and then glances at the window where two of the women with iced coffees look like they'd like to be sipping him up with a straw.

"You should just take off your t-shirt. You know, for sales."

Leo picks up a wet rag and throws it at me.

I catch it in time to avoid getting wet. "Don't bring me into your twisted world. You don't want me competing for their attention." I wink and then place the rag in the sink next to me.

"You do realize that they probably think you're my lover, right?" Leo lifts the dog out of the tub and places him on the grooming table, hooking him up to the pole.

Each woman follows his movements with a head tilt, their mouths ajar slightly.

"You just made them all wet."

"I aim to please." He laughs.

I pop another chip in my mouth and glance over to the room beside us to check on Payne. He's playing with the puppies and having fun.

"Must be hard to be so wanted." My voice is thick with sarcasm because Leo doesn't date. Like ever.

He can thank that bitch Yvette for that. I swear he doesn't even notice anyone with a pussy unless it's an actual pussy cat because I think he sometimes grooms them here. I'm convinced it's why he's okay with the rumor he's gay.

"They like the outside package, that's all." He shrugs.

"Well, they could like the guy on the inside if you ever... I don't know, went out on a date." I catch Payne walking toward the door, stopping to pet another dog.

"We're focusing on you, remember?"

"My life is peachy keen."

"That's why you're screwing the lead actress in your movie." He leans against the wall, crossing his arms, allowing the overhead dryer to finish off the Golden Retriever.

"Don't try to bait me. I'm not fucking her."

"But you want to."

"No."

"Bullshit. I'd bet good money you're having a hard time keeping your hands off her." That know-it-all grin covering his face is making me crazy.

I hop down from the counter. "You have no idea what you're talking about."

"Hold up."

I stop mid-stride.

"Remember it's not just her." His gaze moves to Payne in the other room. "It's them too."

The hint of sadness in Leo's eyes reminds me that he grew up with a single mom. That he probably saw his fair share of dipshits come and go.

"Got it." I nod.

"He really likes you and from what you say he needs a father figure in his life, so don't mess it up."

"Leo." I stop and hold my hand up in the air. "I got it."

"I hope so... now, go buy something." He smiles and I walk out of the grooming area only to have Payne at my feet seconds later.

"Can we buy a dog?" he asks, jumping up and down.

I ruffle his head. "That's your mom's department."

"Pleeease," he whines. His hands are up in a prayer position. "Please?"

"Leo, I'll catch you later man." I give him a half wave which he returns and then I push the door open.

"Please," Payne begs, his footsteps dragging along the pavement.

Spying the ice cream shop a few doors down I figure a distraction might work. "How about some ice cream?"

"Yay! Ice cream."

He grabs my hand and drags me forward toward the placard that has a picture of a giant ice cream cone. "Do they have cookie dough?" he asks, practically vibrating with excitement.

"I dunno, buddy. Let's go take a look."

We step inside and head over to the glass case displaying all the flavors. A sign behind the counter proclaims 'Home of fifty flavors'.

"I can't see," Payne says, tugging on my pant leg.

I bend over and lift him up so that he can see into the freezer. He leans forward as I walk the length of the counter so he can see each and every damn flavor.

"Looks like they have cookie dough, bud. Is that what you want?" He's quiet and doesn't say anything. His expression is serious his brows drawn. "Payne?"

"There's so many." He juts out his bottom lip.

"What can I get you?" the teenaged boy behind the counter asks.

"Can you give us a minute? He's still deciding," I say.

"Sure thing. Just let me know when you're ready." He starts checking the stock of the ice cream buckets, clearly buying time until we're ready.

I look back to Payne. "All right, what's it gonna be?"

"I don't know. Go back that way?" I walk back from

where we came from.

"Again?" I ask after he's still biting his lip and in deep thought. Does this kid never get ice cream that the decision on the kind is this crucial?

I do as he asks and what feels like twenty, but is actually only four minutes later Payne has settled on his original pick of cookie dough.

Note to self: Next time I have to buy a kid ice cream ask for their order and go to the counter *alone*.

"I think we're ready," I say loud enough for the employee to hear me.

He heads over from the other end of the counter, probably as annoyed as I am right now. "What'll it be?"

I set Payne down on his feet and shake my arms out. I might work out on a regular basis, but I don't hold a forty-pound barbell in my arms for five minutes straight.

"Cookie dough, please." I point to the tub in question.

"What size do you want?" he asks.

I look down to Payne. "I want a triple scoop," he says.

I shrug. "Triple scoop it is." It took long enough for the choice of ice cream, we aren't going back and forth on how many scoops.

"You sure about that?" the teenager questions my order.

"You heard the kid," I say and Payne starts cheering and jumping up and down in excitement. Three scoops might be a tad too much, but hey, I'm the Manny. The teenage boy can keep his opinion to himself.

"Okay then." The teenager grabs a cone from the stack and works on assembling Payne's masterpiece.

Once I've paid we head back out onto the street and begin walking toward my truck.

For the first time all day, Payne is silent, mostly because his tongue is working overtime licking at his ice cream. My hand on his back guides him in the right direction.

Five minutes later, halfway to Layla's, Payne is groaning in the back seat so I turn down the radio. "What's wrong buddy?"

"I don't want anymore," he says in an unhappy voice.

I pull onto the freeway and merge with traffic then take a quick glance at him in the rearview mirror. His face is covered in ice cream, dripping from his chin, on his nose and his hands.

"Payne wipe your chin with the napkin that's around the cone, okay?"

"I can't," he says.

"What do you mean you can't?" I ask. "Hold on," I say as I make a hard break. Traffic has slowed to a crawl in the blink of an eye as it's liable to do in L.A. at any given hour.

"I can't because it's wet."

I suck in a breath. Fuck me.

I chance a quick glance in the back seat since we're only moving at about ten miles per hour and immediately wish I didn't. My eyes widen as they take in the ice cream dripping down the cone, over Payne's hand and what's left sitting in his lap.

Shit. I open my center console while keeping an eye on traffic, stopping and going every few seconds. Without taking my gaze from the road I feel around inside and plastic wrappers topple out and onto the floorboards. The box of condoms that I keep in my glove compartment in case of emergencies is open and condom wrappers are scattered inside the glove box and across the floormat below.

*How can a kid his size be so messy?*

Manny fail.

"I'm sticky," Payne half says, half cries.

"Okay, okay. Hang on. Let me think."

"It's all over my privates!" Payne wails and then starts sobbing.

I adjust the rearview mirror so that I can get a better view of him and realize that he's now holding the ice cream cone out to his side so that it's dripping all over my interior.

"Oh, buddy, don't do that. Leave it where it was."

"No! It's cold and sticky," he screams and continues to cry.

"You're going to have to wait until we get back to your place and then we'll get you cleaned up okay?"

I grip the steering wheel harder imagining the state of my interior by the time we reach Layla's in this traffic. I could take the next exit, but by the time I make it across the two lanes of traffic we won't be far from Layla's anyway.

Payne sniffles behind me. I ruined the kid the first day.

"Can't I use one of those?" he asks.

"One of what?" I turn my head quickly to see what he's looking at.

"Those," he says and points with his free hand to the condom wrappers.

"Uh...no, bud. Those are for adults."

"Mommy lets me use her Wet-Naps."

Relief floods my veins that at least he doesn't know what condoms are and won't go telling his mom.

"Oh, those aren't Wet-Naps," I say, hoping he'll drop the subject. I honk my horn at the guy in front of me. Why are there so many damn people in LA?

But of course, he doesn't.

"What are they?" he asks.

I try to think of something to say—something that won't lead to another question and another. I'm at a loss and so finally I say, "You know what? That's also your mom's department."

Thankfully, he accepts my response and goes back to sniffling about his melting ice cream. "Mommy always gets me the kid scoop," he mumbles. "This never happens with Mommy."

I'm a cars length away from sniffling too, thinking of what that sticky liquid is doing to my interior. There's more to this manny stuff than just keeping the kid alive.

————

"Do you like basketball?" I ask Payne, later that afternoon after we've got him all cleaned up.

He shrugs. "Yeah." I glance to the unused mini basketball hoop in the corner of the basement.

We spend most of our time down here, since the majority of his toys are stored in the rec room. Not to mention I figured I'd keep the upstairs clean for the sitter interview.

"Well, my buddy got some tickets for tomorrow night's Lakers game. You wanna go?"

I still remember my very first football game with my dad and my sister, Charlie. It was such a huge deal. He got us the foam fingers, we ate nachos, hamburgers, and had our first taste of Coke. For the record, we thought it was the best thing in the world.

"Sure." He shrugs.

Inside I'm already cringing because I'm not so sure he's going to appreciate the near court seats I snagged.

The doorbell rings and I jog up the stairs. When I open the door, an older woman with gray hair and orthopedic shoes, wearing a dress, stands in the doorway. The interview wasn't scheduled for another half an hour, but I'm going to guess that this is the potential new nanny.

"Hi," I greet her.

She looks me up and down with a disapproving glare. "Are you the dad?"

"Since you rang the doorbell, why don't we start with who you are?"

Her face morphs into disgust, as if her nose could twitch and I'd be turned into a cat or something.

"I'm Nanny Theta." She straightens her back, squares her shoulders, and raises her chin as though she just announced she's the president.

"Come on in, I'm just filling in temporarily." I smile.

She doesn't return the gesture, but walks in with her squeaky brown canoe feet.

"Is Layla here?" Her gaze sweeps around the foyer.

Payne runs in and slides on the marble floors, skidding to a stop by my legs. He wraps his arms around, hiding behind my legs.

"This is Payne." I pat his back.

"Come here, boy, let me see you." She crosses her arm, her small shell purse in front of her now.

Payne grips my jeans tighter.

"He can be shy," I say.

He's never really been so with me, but it's clear that he wants nothing to do with this woman.

"You should never use that word. It only makes them believe it's okay." Her attention is still focused where Payne is strung around my legs. "Payne, you need to unglue yourself and step forward for presentation."

"Why don't we move into the family room and get better acquainted? Give him some time to warm up." I motion in the direction of the family room, hoping she'll go first.

"Have it your way, but babying him is not going to help him with social anxiety. I'm a firm believer that you cannot treat them as children, otherwise they never grow up."

She runs her finger along the table set against the foyer wall as we pass before stepping into the family room.

*What is her problem? I think Nanny Theta might belong more in the military than looking after young children.*

"A clean and orderly house helps with behavioral problems. She'll have to hire a housemaid. I do *not* dust, or vacuum. I don't prepare dinners. I'm here for the children's care only." She stands in the middle of the room, her arms crossed and her judgmental eyes taking in every surface of the house.

Payne scurries further behind my legs than before.

"That should really wait until Layla is here. Let me text her and see when she's due back."

"Her tardiness is not a good sign," she snips.

"I'm pretty sure you're early."

Her head twists fast and abruptly, her eyes glaring. "Being early is being on time. I'm sure she wouldn't like it if I was late."

I release an annoyed breath. This woman is horrendous. "Please take a seat and we'll be right back."

She pats the cushion, brushing something away with her hand, and then sits on the edge of the couch.

I pull my phone out, but the front door opens and Layla comes barreling in, an exhausted look on her face.

"Is that minivan her?" she asks, with Via propped on her hip.

I've never been attracted to a woman because she's holding a baby, but there's something about Layla when Via is plastered to her side that makes me want to kiss her.

"Yeah." I hold out my arms, hoping to take Via from her so she can interview the dragon lady.

I smile wide, but Via's hand clings to her mom's blouse, popping a button open and granting me a glimpse at her red, lacy bra. My dick shifts in my pants and so I do the same to try to hide the evidence.

"It's okay, I'll just do it with her." She runs into the other room before I have a chance to tell her about her blouse.

At first all I hear are their muffled introductions, but then Layla calls for Payne.

He shakes his head frantically at me, begging me with his eyes not to send him in there.

"It's okay, just go." I nudge him forward a little but his feet stop. "I'll go with you."

I push him forward, his legs straight, his socks sliding on the hardwood floors. Layla widens her eyes at us when we enter the room.

"He's just being ..." I start.

"Shy," Layla says, finishing my sentence.

"I already told him that that word is a terrible word to use in front of children," Nanny Theta says. "It makes the boy—"

"Think that shyness is appropriate," I say. "Nanny Theta also doesn't believe in treating them like children."

I sit down and Payne plops down next to me. This woman will chew sweet Layla up and spit her out, so I feel like it's my duty to stay.

"I have to admit, usually Payne is the opposite of... timid?" Layla says, and the swell of her breasts steals all my attention because her button is still undone.

"Layla, dear." Nanny Theta leans forward, whispering something to her.

Whatever she says, Layla's eyes shoot my way and then she places Via on the couch and, with pink cheeks, buttons up her blouse, shooting me a look. Not a look of displeasure though. It feels more flirtatious, as if what she'd really like to do is undo another button.

Nanny Theta is a no-go. She's a cockblocker.

Via climbs down from the couch and walks over to the ball popper I fixed the other day. She makes a few noises to get my attention, which I ignore in the interests of moving this interview along and getting this horrid woman out of Layla's home. Payne falls to the ground to play with his sister, but Via ignores him, pulling at the calf of my jeans.

"That is enough." Nanny Theta claps her hands. "You."

She points to me. "Take that toy and the children into the other room."

*Who does this lady think she is?*

Layla is pursing her lips and I can't tell if she's trying not to laugh or if she's just displeased with the other woman's outburst.

"Sure, let's go, kids." I pick up the toy and Payne holds Via's hand on the way out.

We're not in the other room for more than fifteen minutes and Payne is playing with Via, mimicking what I usually do by taking the balls and hiding them in his hands.

The script is still on the table since I'd been working on it after Payne passed out on the way home from Leo's dog salon, so I organize the papers and place them on top of my computer. I might be the only thirty-four-year-old who prefers a printout over a virtual version.

"What do you think of Nanny Theta?" I ask Payne.

"I don't like her." He scrunches up his face in a way that reminds me of his mother.

"Yeah, hopefully your mom has some other options before Monday."

Payne continues to play with Via for a few more minutes. He picks up the ball and starts running all over the room, then weaves into the kitchen. Via is chasing him the entire time, screaming and laughing and wanting it back.

"Via, here." I hold up another ball, but she shakes her head and eyes Payne again.

He jumps from kitchen chair to kitchen chair and Via continues to scream. He runs into the family room before I can stop him and Via follows. I hop up and run into the room, but Payne is jumping on the chair. Layla has her hand on his arm, scolding him, but he's not listening to her. He throws the ball at Via's head and she falls down on her butt, crying hysterically. If all that isn't enough, Payne escapes his mom's hold and jumps off the couch, picking up magazines and throwing them on the ground. He moves to the wicker basket of toys, tossing every toy out of the basket.

"See, this is more than just nannying, Miss Andrews. Just as I thought, he has a behavioral disorder. Allow me to show you how I deal with it." Nanny Theta stands from the couch faster than I would have thought possible. Those orthopedic shoes must be working for her.

She grabs Payne by the arm, yanks him up and places her finger in his face, scolding him for his behavior. Unfortunately, she's no match for Payne. He moves his arm out of her hold and then rears it back.

"No, Payne!" Layla says right before he smacks Nanny Theta across the cheek.

Silence erupts into the room. Even Via, who is now in my arms, is silent.

"Well, I... I've never ..." Nanny Theta grabs Payne and turns him around, her own hand cocked and ready to spank Payne.

Layla rushes over and grabs her wrist. "Don't you lay one hand on my son."

I've seen a lot of sides of Layla in the past week, but this is a new one. A scary one. Don't piss this woman off.

Nanny Theta stands poised with her arm out. "He's a deviant." Spittle flies from her yellow-stained teeth.

"He's a child. One who needs guidance. That's our jobs as adults. Now please leave my house."

"You aren't doing him any favors." Layla lets go and Nanny Theta drops her arm. Payne immediately darts behind Layla's back. "He's never going learn to behave if you don't use physical discipline."

"I wish I could say this was a pleasant visit. You aren't the person I want watching my child all day." Layla follows her to the door, and Payne crawls into the corner of the couch.

"I don't understand this new generation," Nanny Theta says and a second later Layla has slammed the door behind her.

I can see in her eyes that she's about to lose it and on the verge of crying.

I continue to bounce Via in my arms to keep her content when she starts hiccupping.

"Vance. Um, give her to me." Layla is narrowing the distance between us, her hands out.

"I got this. Go take a minute."

She shakes her head. "Just pass her over."

Her fingertips are on Via, ready to pluck her out of my arms, when Via unloads and pukes all over me.

●12

## Layla

The doorbell rings and I glance back and forth between the door and Vance.

"Go," he directs me and disappears around the corner with Via in his arms.

I answer the door and Nanny Theta is standing on the porch, her shoulders high, nose even higher.

"My purse," she says like I'm her servant.

I slam the door—and take great pleasure in doing so, I might add—then walk into the family room where Payne is still pressing his face into one of the cushions. Grabbing her purse, I walk back to the front door, toss her purse to her and slam the door again.

Pushing all that behind me, I sit on the couch next to Payne, wrapping my arm around his shoulders. His back is heaving and I can just make out his small cries, even though they're muffled from the pillow.

"Why did you act like that?" I ask, more concerned than angry.

He twists his entire body away from me.

"Payne." I sigh. "Tell me."

He peeks his head up and I dip my own down to get his attention.

"I don't like her."

"Okay, but you could have waited until after she left and talked to me." I pull him close and gradually slide the pillow out from in between us.

He curls into my side. "I like Vance," he says with a sniff.

I nod, already knowing that's what this is really about. "I know, but Vance isn't a qualified nanny. He has a job. We have to find someone else."

He's quiet and I know this is hard for him. "Hey." I draw back to look into his eyes. "Why don't we find someone together, okay? We'll both have a say in who it is."

His lips tip up a bit and he nods.

"Okay, I have to check on Vance and Via. Via threw up on him."

Payne's eyes widen.

"Yep. Let's go help Vance."

I walk up the stairs with Payne at my side.

"Mom?" he asks.

I stop at the top of the staircase. "Yes?"

"Do you like Vance?"

I refrain from telling my four-year-old just how much I like Vance and how certain parts of me seem to *really* like him more than others.

"I do. He's a nice guy."

"Can we get a dog?" He changes subjects so quick it takes me a second to wrap my head around the change of direction this conversation is taking.

"No, not right now."

"I knew you'd say no." He frowns and stomps off toward his sister's room.

We enter, finding no one there, so we head toward her

bathroom. My feet halt the moment I see them and my jaw drops.

*Am I drooling?*

Vance is bare-chested, his hard chest, biceps and six-pack on display. As if that didn't get me wet enough, he even took the time to give Via a quick bath and put her in a clean diaper.

"I think my shirt is toast." He glances to the garbage can, where his shirt and all of Via's clothes are.

"I can probably wash it out." *On your washboard abs*, I don't add.

My hand moves for the can, but he slides it out of my reach. "Nah, I don't need it."

"Payne, can you take Via and get her pajamas out?" I say, my eyes not leaving Vance's.

Vance gently places Via on the ground and Payne holds her hand as they walk out.

"I might have one of Carver's shirts hanging around."

Vance shakes his head. "Nah, I'd rather not wear the shirt of the man you love."

"Loved. I loved him. Past tense."

He nods his head. "Yeah, well, if it's all the same, I'll just put my jacket on when I leave."

The thought of a shirtless Vance in my house for any period of time has me wanting to press my thighs together to relieve the ache.

"Come. I must have something for you to wear." I grab his hand and lead him out of the bathroom, into Via's bedroom, where I promptly drop his hand.

*The kids. I am the worst mother. I almost forgot they were here for a second.*

I put Via in her pajamas as quick as my hands will work. Then I realize I've yet to feed them dinner. I'm slowly losing my mind having this man so near.

"Payne, I'm going to find a shirt for Vance. Can you change into your pajamas and play with Via in your room?"

Payne smiles. "Sure."

"Way to be helpful, buddy." Vance ruffles his hair in the same way I do sometimes.

Payne's smile widens further and he takes his sister by the hand and goes into his room.

Once they're gone, Vance leans into me, his mouth only inches from my ear. "I'm ready to see *your* bedroom, Layla," he whispers and I'm unable to stop the shiver that runs up my spine.

I turn on the balls of my feet and he's so near. Like some Pavlovian response I swear I can taste the mint from his mouth from a few nights ago. Without another word I take off toward my bedroom, aware of the fact that he's watching my every move from behind. By the time we reach my closet, every nerve in my body is on high alert.

I open one of the drawers, knowing I must have a t-shirt of some sort that's way too big for me.

His arm circles my waist and he twists me around, pushing my back into the wall of dresser drawers in my walk-in. His lips crash down onto mine and just like the other night, our mouths begin their own chaotic, desperate dance as we attempt to get enough of one another. He still tastes minty and I know I'll never chew a picce of gum without feeling the safety of his arms around me.

"Jesus, Layla, I can't stop myself," he murmurs before his lips sear a path from my jaw to my ear. He grinds himself into me. "Feel this? Every time you're around, I'm as hard as fucking steel."

I do feel it and it only makes me moan and grind harder against him. "Vance." I bite his earlobe and his breathing picks up pace in my ear.

His hand slides up the front of my blouse, grabbing one

breast, tearing down the cup of my bra, and his thumb brushes across my nipple.

My head falls back and he takes the opportunity to rain kisses down my exposed throat.

"More. I need more," I whisper, sinking my fingers into his hair and holding his head to me.

He unbuttons my blouse and his light beard scratches my skin on the path down, the feeling a heady mix of too much sensation and not quite enough. Without warning, his mouth encases my breast and he twirls my nipple around with his tongue like his own plaything until my fingers are digging into his scalp. There's a fire burning so strong between my legs, I'll need a fire hose to douse it. Vance and his hose are perfect for the job.

His tongue on my nipple slows and he rests his chin on my bare breast, staring up at me. "I think we'll have to continue this another time," he says in a deep, throaty voice.

"I know. My vibrator is going to have its work cut out for it tonight." I laugh and his lips cast small kisses all the way up until he's right in front of my face.

"Why don't you get comfortable and put on a pair of leggings." He winks, his lips meeting mine one more time. "And no panties." He turns back around to leave my closet.

"Vance. You know we shouldn't." I'm voicing the words I should be saying, but everything about them feels wrong.

Walking backwards toward the door, he chuckles. "I won't tell if you don't." The smirk I've become so used to rests on his lips as he disappears.

One little secret never hurt anyone, right?

———

SOMEHOW, I survive dinner with the kids even with the fact that every time I pass Vance when the kids aren't paying attention, his hand slides over my ass. Thankfully, he agreed to wear a t-shirt I had that was too big for me. If his delicious abs had been on display I don't know what I would have done.

"Time for bed!" I clap my hands and Vance laughs.

Payne whines. "Can Vance read me my book?" he asks and I glance over to where Vance is sitting on the chair.

"I'd love to." Vance hops up and follows Payne out of the room.

I pick up Via and we follow behind.

While I rock Via and read her *Goodnight Moon*, I hear Vance and Payne laughing about a shark book Payne hasn't been able to get enough of lately.

Via's hand moves up to my hair and then she caresses my face.

"What do you think, baby? Is Mommy crazy?"

She smiles over her pacifier with her hand resting on my bare skin. I watch her for a few minutes until her eyes drift closed and her hand falls from my face.

I stand up and place her in the crib, turning on her twilight light, and leave the room, closing the door softly behind me.

With Vance still reading to Payne, I head downstairs. Mostly because I don't trust myself to wait for him in the hallway. I have no doubt we'd end up in my bed within five minutes.

By the time Vance makes it downstairs, I've poured myself a glass of white wine and placed an open beer on the coffee table for him.

"You're snooping." He falls down beside me onto the couch, grabbing the beer in the same motion.

"Just looking." I place his script back down on his computer.

"I'm kidding. It's okay." He sits up, resting his elbows on

his knees, so near that his crisp cologne lights every nerve ending in my body.

I pick it back up. "How is it going?" His chicken-scratch handwriting is written in some of the margins, but for some reason it makes the script more him, and it feels more intimate that it's here in my house.

"It's okay. I meet with a script manager next week. Jagger set it up."

"What are you changing? I think it's awesome as is." I lean back into the couch, propping my feet up on the table. "Actually, there is one scene I think needs a little tweaking."

"And what's that?" he asks, a smile teasing his lips.

"You're probably thinking that I should stay out of it... that I'm only an actress." I raise my eyebrows and he chuckles.

"You caught me, but I want to hear it. What scene?"

I flip through the pages to reach the scene where Melanie and Joseph have sex after one of the heists. "I think you need to add romance into this one." I tap my finger on the page.

"Romance? They're outlaws." He tips his beer back and then places it on the table, grabbing his pencil and leaning in close. "Where?"

"After they get off the yacht with all the jewels, you have Joseph pin her against the hotel window, stripping her down and taking her from behind."

Damn. I shouldn't have listened to Vance and not worn any underwear because my yoga pants are now wet.

"You don't like that scene?" He raises his brow and that cocky smirk is on his face.

We both know how sexy the scene is.

"Oh, I like it, but I'd rather him press her against the window, strip her down and then carry her off to the bed to make love to her with the jewels spread out all over the bed."

He plucks the paper from me, his pencil poised. "You

think Joseph doesn't love her because he fucks her against the window?"

Oh, my God, the way he says 'fuck' makes me want to run to my nightstand and grab my Unicorn Cock vibrator and go to town. Instead, I take a deep breath and explain what I mean.

"I think he loves her, but I think this is a pivotal point to show her because they were almost hurt. Well, Melanie was anyway, and I think he'd be vulnerable to her at this point. When you stare death in the eye, you tend to hold the ones you love tighter. Like when I hear a kid has gone missing or heaven forbid something happened, I tend to keep Payne and Via close right after. I'm constantly kissing them and telling them how much I love them. I think Joseph would do the same thing. Realize how much she means to him and cherish her."

He's busy jotting notes down in the margin.

"I like it and I see your point." He places the script down with his pencil, leaning toward me. "Tell me, Ms. Andrews, do you see anything else that needs tweaking?"

"No."

*I only see you.*

But I don't say that. I can't.

His hand skims up the inside of my thigh. "Tell me, Layla, what do you want?" he whispers, his breath tickling my ear.

*You!* I want to scream, but instead remain quiet, allowing his hand to cup my pussy though my leggings.

"I don't know," I say in a breathy voice, just as he pushes one finger into me through the fabric.

My body tenses, my back arches, and I suck in a quick breath.

"You think we should keep this professional?" he asks as his finger runs up and down the seam of my leggings.

"Yes."

"I agree. Should I stop then?"

My head is screaming yes, but he knows I'm like a bee to a soda can when it comes to him. I hover and hover and somehow, I'm not able to resist the lure even though I know it's a trap. I'll dive in eventually, knowing it's sure to cause me pain.

"I think we should talk about the ramifications of our actions."

He places an open-mouthed kiss on my neck. "Ramifications?" His fingers are conducting some sort of symphony that has my body humming. "I like you, Layla, and I think you like me too."

Through the fabric of my yoga pants, he finds my clit and all his attention focuses on the small nub, alight with a million nerve endings searching for release.

"I do like you. A lot," I manage to squeak out.

"Then let me take care of you. I want to feel you come all over my hand."

With the one statement I lose the battle to fight.

My back is arched, and through the thin fabric of my t-shirt and yoga pants, Vance nips at my breasts. His fingers strum my pussy like he's a Grammy-winning guitarist. Eventually his fingers push past the waistband of my leggings and the skin-to-clit contact is almost more than I can take. His lips capture mine in a slow kiss that matches the movements of his actions below. My orgasm climbs like a diver swimming up to the surface of the water. It's not a fast release, not explosive. He slowly and steadily brings me higher and higher until I bite down on his lower lip with a long growl of pleasure.

Even after it's clear my orgasm finished, Vance's hand moulds to my hip and he continues to make out with me until we're both out of breath.

"Are you relaxed now?" he asks, staring down at me.

"Like spaghetti."

He laughs, kissing my lips one more time. "Then I did my job."

He sits straight up, the weight of him gone, and it immediately brings a feeling of loss.

"Let me repay you." I get on my knees, about to straddle him.

"Not tonight." He packs his stuff and stands. "You need to get some sleep. I'll see you tomorrow morning."

Well, this seems weird, but okay. I've never had a guy give me pleasure and not expect something in return. Not that I have all that much experience since I met Carver on the set of the family sitcom we both worked on as kids, but still.

I follow him to the door, and he strips the shirt off his body and puts on his jacket.

"You can keep it," I say.

His hand moves around my neck and he pulls me to him, his mouth commanding my full attention. I'm certain my knees weaken, but he keeps me held up.

"My buddy is having a barbecue on the beach this weekend," he says. "Any chance you'd want to come?"

Is he asking me on a date? I'm positively giddy inside.

I bite my lip and nod.

He takes his thumb and pushes my lip down. "Keep doing that and I'll never leave."

"You can stay."

He chuckles. "Nope. You are getting some sleep. Good night, Layla."

"Good night."

The door shuts and my heart opens.

Damn him.

## 13

### Vance

The bonfire is already going, and unlike Jagger, who would invite two hundred people to a shindig he was throwing, Leo's kept the guest list small for the barbecue.

Grabbing a beer from the bucket, I sit in a beach chair looking out at the ocean when two hands cover my eyes.

"Guess who?" a high-pitched female voice sounds in my ear.

The small set of hands come off my eyes and I stand up and turn around.

*Kali.*

She throws herself in my arms. "Bet you missed me," she whispers and her hand slides down my back to grab my ass.

I take a step back. "Hey, Kali." I take a swig of my beer. Why the hell is she here? She's not even a close friend of Leo's.

"What kind of hello is that?" she asks with a false smile on her face.

I should warn you now. I've slept with Kali. Once. And I was very drunk. Since then she thinks we're soul mates or some shit, even though it's been almost a year and I've never been a repeat offender with her.

"I'm expecting someone." Honesty is always best, right? I push from my mind the fact that I haven't been completely honest with Layla.

"Expecting someone?" She wrinkles her nose. "What does that mean?"

"It means I invited someone to meet me here tonight."

Just as I say that my phone vibrates in my pocket. I pull it out and see Layla's name on the screen.

Last night after I left, I texted her the address. Maybe she's having trouble finding it or something.

"Hey," I say.

"Bad news. Babysitter bailed."

"You have so many sitter problems." I walk away from Kali toward the edge of the ocean and look around. A few of Leo's friends have kids and although that will mean an early night for Layla, a few hours with her is better than nothing. "Bring them."

"I think we'll take a rain check." Disappointment is clear in her voice so I push a little more.

"Have I never told you? I don't have a rain check policy. It's now or never." I curl my toes in the sand beneath my feet, waiting for her response.

"Well, that's sad because it's a never right now."

"Until Monday, you mean?" I laugh since after Nanny Theta, I told Layla I'd do another week or two until she can find someone suitable. Really, she just needs someone for when we start filming my script, which won't be for a while.

She giggles and the sound makes me wish I could see the look on her face while she's doing that, witness the delight that must be present in her eyes. "Yeah, I guess so. But have fun tonight. We'll plan something another time."

"No. Come on. I'll help you with the kids."

"I'm not sure... I thought your house was all breakable?" She throws the words from when she first asked me to be her nanny back at me.

"Now that I love them so much, I'm okay with it. Get in the car and get over here. Besides, we'll pretty much be on the beach anyway."

She releases a breath. "Okay. Let me get them ready."

"I'll be waiting."

"If you're smart you'll be Payne-proofing your house." She hangs up and I tuck my phone back in my pocket.

One of the other kids throws a ball and I manage to see it coming in my peripheral vision and catch it before it hits me in the head.

He comes over and I hand it over to him.

"Thanks, Vance."

"You're welcome." It's then I realize I have no idea what that kid's name is and he's always at Leo's parties.

He smiles and runs away, kicking the football back to his brother.

I stand there wondering why it bothers me now, the realization that I was too self-absorbed before to care about learning his name. What's changed?

It's a stupid question because it's already becoming clear to me that Layla's presence in my life is starting to change everything—whether I want it to or not.

———

AN HOUR LATER, I'm waiting outside for Layla and the kids, drinking my beer and sitting on the stairs to our condo building. I've lived here since I moved to Los Angeles. I can certainly afford better at this stage of my life, but for some reason I've never had the urge to move. It's a great complex right on the beach, the rent isn't astronomical, and the tenants are all pretty cool.

But I know that's not the reason I stay. It's because it's familiar and holds a lot of good memories. It's where Leo, Jagger and myself first met—sharing one of the units together while Jagger's family was in a short period of cutting him off the purse strings. We've been friends for over a decade and in a lot of ways we all grew into men together. In the years since we first shared a place both Leo and myself have moved into our own units as apartments came up in the complex, and Jagger has moved on to his high-rise condo and Malibu pad, but we're all still tight.

As I sit there reminiscing to myself, I try to ignore how antsy I feel to see her. I don't understand what's happened. How can a woman pique my interest in such a short time? I haven't even slept with her, and not because she didn't want to. I'm hesitant to cross that line because I actually *like* this woman. A lot.

A black SUV rolls slowly down the street and stops in front of me. The driver exits the vehicle and opens up the back door. I should have realized she'd call for a car.

Layla steps out wearing a pair of tight jeans, a blouse, and jean jacket. She unstraps Via and holds her, while Payne climbs out on his own.

"Thanks, Miles. I'll call you in a few hours." She shuts the door and the three of them walk toward me.

"Hey, guys." I high-five Payne and Via, who just keeps slapping my hand.

"Are you sure about this?" Layla looks apprehensive.

"Of course. The party is low-key, no press or anything."

She nods, but I figure it's better to get her into the back—someone could have followed her.

We head through the courtyard in the center of all the

units and reach the beach. Payne immediately runs toward the other kids and joins in with them, kicking the ball.

"Oh, boy." Layla tenses next to me when she spots how many people are here and her gaze fixes on Payne.

I place my hand on the small of her back and lean in. "Relax. I promise, everyone is good people and they won't be taking pictures and selling them to the tabloids."

She nods a few times. "Okay, I'll try."

"Now, give me Via and let's get you a drink." Via actually comes to me when I put my hands out for her and I pretend we're flying away before settling her on my side.

Jagger is sitting on the beach chair and we have to pass him as we make our way to the cooler.

"Layla, you got Vance to hold a baby?" he says when he sees us. His eyebrow is so far cocked you'd think he had lessons from Dr. Evil in *Austin Powers*.

"Hi, Jagger," Layla says softly. "This is my daughter, Via."

"That's an usual name," he says.

"It's actually Olivia, but ever since she was little Via just stuck."

"How cute." Jagger looks between the two of us, his usual smile absent.

"Why don't you go get a drink, Jagger?"

"I have a beer," he says, holding it up in front of him and pinning me with a stare.

"Then just go," I tell him and his sour mood.

"I can't be the only one out of the three of us who thinks this is a bad idea."

"What's a bad idea?" I ask him.

"You guys playing house, that's what." He shakes his head like a disappointed father.

"Here." I pass Via to Layla. "Can you excuse us for a minute? I'll join you in a sec."

"Sure." Layla walks toward Payne, but Leo quickly cuts her off. At least he seems more welcoming than Jagger.

"Cut the shit, Vance. I told you to stay away from her." Jagger's voice is laced with anger and I kick myself for not giving him a heads-up before I invited her.

"Relax. Nothing's really going on. We're just having fun."

"No." He shakes his head and points the tip of his beer at me. "You think you're having fun. She thinks you're going to be a substitute daddy to her kids."

"She knows this is nothing serious. The last thing she wants is a serious relationship right now." I down half my beer.

"I don't understand why you need to play with fire. You'd think you'd learned your lesson after that whole mess with Gwen, but here we go again. You know what?" He raises his hand in the air. "Do what you want. Ruin this opportunity. I hope she's worth it."

"You two are looking entirely too serious. This is a party!" Kali waggles her manicured nails between us, her hips swinging at the same speed as her finger, slow and seducing.

"Go away, Kali," I say, my eyes fixed on Jagger.

"Oh, look, another one of your mistakes is here tonight." Jagger shakes his head and stands, walking away.

"What does that mean?" Kali's valley girl voice does nothing to remove her name from my list of mistakes.

"He's just an asshole," I mumble and turn around and see Layla talking with Leo, while Via is petting Cooper and laughing every time he sniffs her. A smile graces my lips until Kali swings her small thin arm around my neck, pulling me toward her and kissing my cheek.

Of course, Layla's gaze shoots my way at that exact moment, because that's my life lately.

I move Kali off me. "I told you I'm here with someone."

Technically, I'm not *with* Layla, but Kali needs to know her place and that place is not cuddled up next to me.

"Layla Andrews? I heard she and Carver are getting back together," she says to my retreating back.

"Don't believe everything you read," I toss back over my shoulder, hoping she'll just go the fuck away.

So far this is not how I pictured my night going.

"Old girlfriend?" Layla asks when I bend down to join Via and Cooper.

"Kali? No, she just lives in the building," Leo says, thankfully leaving out the part about me sleeping with her.

"She looks like she wants to be more than just a neighbor," Layla comments, her eyes clearly questioning me, but it's her smile that confuses me. She seems as if she couldn't care either way.

Fuck. Why does her lack of jealousy bother me?

"I have my own neighbor. Of course, I think he's more of a peeping tom. I can guarantee he's sold more than one bikini photo to the tabloids." She's all smiles, as though we're just friends and I didn't make her come with my hand the other night.

Someone calls Leo over and Cooper follows, which makes Via follow, and soon Layla and I are walking behind to keep an eye on her.

"You should file an order of protection. Get a higher fence or something."

She laughs. "It's okay, I think he's more of an admirer than anything. He's harmless."

"Doesn't sound like it," I murmur under my breath as I try to calm down my own rage from the thought of some creep hiding in the bushes to get pictures of her.

"One day I'll make it big and afford a mansion with a gate and tons of acres and I won't need to worry about it." She elbows me. "Maybe your film will be the one to make that happen. We can have side-by-side mansions. Then I can drop off the kids whenever I have a hot date." She laughs.

I try to ignore how much her comment irks me—because wasn't I just insisting to Jagger that whatever *this* is between us is just fun and games?—and tip my head back and take the last swig of my beer. "Yeah, call me Manny for life." With my beer empty, I figure I might as well enjoy another, since the rest of my evening will not involve my becoming more familiar with Layla's anatomy.

"I'll be right back. You good?" I ask.

She smiles. "Yeah. I have the kids so this will be it for me tonight."

I leave her to grab another beer and dispose of my old one and admittedly to pull my shit together.

I'm halfway to my destination when a scream comes from behind me. I turn back around to find Payne holding his leg and crying. Layla swoops Via up and runs toward Payne, falling to her knees on the sand to assess the situation. I'm sure Layla can handle it, but I find myself headed in their direction.

Leo and Jagger both meet me there, Cooper at Leo's side. The dog now has Via's undivided attention.

"It's a pretty big gash," Leo says. "Let's take him inside and get it cleaned up."

"I've got it," I tell them and pick up Payne.

"I can take care of this. I'll call Miles back," Layla offers.

"Let's get him cleaned off first and then we'll see."

"No, Mom, I'm having fun," Payne whines.

"Fucking dipshits!" Jagger stomps off in the sand toward a group of twentysomethings a little farther down. "No glass on the beach. What are you, morons?"

"Hey, Jagger, lay off on the swearing." Layla turns with Via in her arms.

"Shit. Sorry, Layla," he tosses over his shoulder as he strides away.

"Impressive, I've never heard Jagger take instruction from a female before," Leo says with a laugh. "I doubt it even was those kids, but he has a point. Why people bring glass to a beach I have no idea."

"I'm sure Payne will be fine. He's not even crying anymore," she says.

"I'd like to know for sure. Coop will keep your little one busy."

Layla looks back and smiles. "You guys are so sweet. The three of you are good friends?"

"Yeah, but I'm the sweetest," Leo says, raising his shoulders and scrunching his nose in a what-are-you-going-to-do kinda way.

When we reach my condo, I place Payne on the kitchen counter.

"Let me grab the first-aid kit." I go head toward my bathroom.

"Have you had other scripts sell?" Layla asks loud enough for me to hear her. Her question is immediately followed by a laugh from Leo.

I tense as I'm rifling through the cabinet. How is it that I keep forgetting about the secret I'm keeping from her?

"I figured you lived in more of a studio," she says when I return to the kitchen.

I shrug. "It's only a two-bedroom condo."

"On the beach." She looks thoroughly confused, but turns to Leo. "What do you do?"

"He dresses up dogs in tutus and dresses," I say, as I wipe down Payne's shin.

"If children weren't present, I'd have some choice words for you," Leo chimes in. "I own Canine Couture."

Layla's entire face lights up. "No way. Really?" She beelines it to the couch where Via is hugging Cooper so close to her I wonder if the dog can breathe. "My one make-up artist for the movie I'm filming has two toy poodles and she was raving about your stuff just last week. Says she's been following you for years."

I place the Band-Aid on Payne. "Better?"

Payne nods and I help him down from the counter. "Mom, can I go back outside? Can I, Mom? Please?"

Layla raises her finger.

"Mom!" Payne screams.

"Payne, wait for her to finish, buddy," I say and place my hand on his shoulder.

He stays quiet, but his feet start tapping and his arms start flailing as if he can barely contain the energy inside him wanting to burst out.

"That's nice to hear," Leo says. "How about I take Payne back downstairs while you clean this up, Vance?"

Leo moves toward the door, causing Cooper to follow, and Via whines as soon as he's out of her grasp.

"I can take the little one, too," Leo offers.

Layla glances back at me. "I have to go to the bathroom really quick. How about I clean up and then you can go with to watch the kids?"

"I like to think kids are like dogs. I can watch more than one at once. I'll take them to the beach and keep a close eye."

Layla bites her lip and her cheeks tinge pink. "Um..."

"Leo's a good one," I say. "Plus, we'll be five minutes tops."

Layla nods, though a little unsure.

Leo takes the dog and two kids out of the condo, while I move to the sink to clean up and explain where the bathroom is to Layla.

Minutes later, the bathroom door opens. I'm leaning against my counter with my arms folded over my chest.

"Thanks for taking care of Payne," she says. "You ready?"

She passes me, but I grab her wrist and pull her back. "Why were you acting like that out there?"

Her eyes dim and I regret saying anything. "Like what?"

"Like I didn't get you off the other night."

She laughs. "Aren't we just having fun?" she asks, her tone suggesting she's feeling me out. "Not to mention Kali. I mean, how dense do you think I am? I thought you had more class than to invite me to a party with a girl you fucked around with in attendance."

"Whoa, what the hell?"

*Talk about a one-eighty. First, she doesn't care and now she's jealous?*

She raises her hand. "I'm sorry. Forget I said anything. Fooling around with each other is a mistake. Let's just quit while we're ahead."

She tries to walk away but I pull her toward me again. "We're not ahead until you've been underneath me." I crash my lips down to hers.

## 14

## Layla

I let him kiss me.

What am I saying? I kiss him back. Just as fiercely and powerfully as he's doing to me.

Once we're both panting and moaning into each other's mouths, he tears his lips from mine. "Kali's no one. Yes, we were together once, but it was a mistake I regretted immediately." Then his lips are on mine again.

I try to turn my face away, but he holds my head in his hands, licking up my throat. "Who's to say you won't regret this?" I ask in a breathy voice.

He ceases all movement and rears back to look into my eyes. "I'm not going to regret this, Layla. I've wanted you since I first saw you outside that trailer."

He cups my breasts and I arch to give him better access. "God, Vance, I want you so bad, but we can't do this. Jagger is right. We're committing career suicide."

"Jagger's an ass. We're adults. If it doesn't work out, we'll figure it out, right?" He tries to kiss me, but I keep dodging his mouth.

"I don't know."

Finally, he stops all movement, pulling away enough to lock gazes with me. "Do you not want me?" he asks, seeming almost offended.

"Yes, I want you."

"Then let's just see how it goes. I promise I won't fire you if you break my heart. And you won't quit the film if I break yours. Deal?"

My head wars with my heart. I know this isn't a good idea, but on the flipside, how is working alongside Vance while trying to deny my attraction for him going to play out? Not only will it be distracting, it'll be pure hell.

The way I figure it, I'm damned if I do and damned if I don't.

I look straight into his eyes. "Deal. Now do that thing with your tongue again."

His cocky smile appears and he takes ownership of my mouth once again.

"Fucking shit. You guys are idiots." Jagger's voice permeates our fog and he slams the door shut behind him and heads down the hall to the bathroom.

I can't help but start laughing, which draws our kiss to a close.

"Told you he's an asshole," Vance grumbles.

"He's going to give you hell." I poke him in the chest.

"Let him. Think the kids are tired?"

I chuckle, knowing exactly what's on his mind. "Yeah, but maybe I should feed them first."

"Food coma? I love the sound of that."

A giddiness envelops me when he takes my hand, leading me toward the door.

I take in where he lives, where he sleeps, watches television, where he relaxes. It's all glass, chrome and hardwood with a wide span of windows overlooking the ocean. The building itself isn't too flashy, but the inside of this place screams money.

"Seriously, Vance, this is a really nice condo. Do you sell a lot of scripts?"

He stops and turns around, placing each of his hands on my cheeks. "You know what? We need to talk." The smile disappears from his face and instead of leading me toward the door, he guides me to the couch.

He's a trust-fund baby? No problem.

He sells his body at night? It could be worse, right?

Maybe he's a thief? Robbed a few banks.

I'm totally overthinking this.

I sit there, my leg bouncing anxiously as I wait for him to start speaking.

"I wanted to tell you this before, but I didn't think it was a major deal. If we're going to be togeth—"

The door swings open and a long-annoyed breath leaves Vance's lips.

"Um... she fell asleep." Leo is holding Via in his arms with Cooper and Payne at his side.

I give Vance a look, but he's already moving toward the door. I step up and take my sleeping princess from Leo.

"Call Miles. I don't have a car seat for Via. I'll meet you at your place," Vance says.

"What? The party is just beginning." Leo holds out his hands at his sides. "You can't leave."

"Next time I'll get a babysitter, promise." I hold Via to my chest and Leo nods, his dark blonde hair falling over his forehead with the movement.

"I'll plan another one soon." He walks out with Cooper following right behind him. Seriously, I need someone as loyal and committed to me as that.

Even though I try not to get my hopes up, I secretly can't help but hope that Vance is the man for the job.

———

VIA STAYS ASLEEP DURING TRANSPORT, but I had to stop and grab Payne a hamburger.

Don't judge. I haven't gotten laid in a year and even then, it was a typical Carver flash fuck. Something tells me that Vance knows his way around a woman's body and I plan for him to take his time.

Payne is out of the bath and changing into his pajamas when the doorbell rings.

"I'll be right back, sweetie, finish up." I jog down the stairs, wishing I had time to freshen up. My hair probably smells like campfire and I'm pretty sure I have a thin layer of beach sand all over me. Although as luck—or maybe premeditation—would have it, I shaved this morning.

I open the door to find Vance's hands stuffed into his pockets, his smile reaching all the way up to his caramel eyes. I could become addicted to that look.

"Hey." His voice is suave and smooth and all my insides turn into goo.

"Hi. I'm just finishing up with Payne. Give me five." I hold my fingers up and run back up the stairs. Right before I disappear I look back and find him staring at my ass.

"What can I say, I like the view." He winks and then heads into the family room.

God, I might actually die of heart failure from the way it's pitter-pattering so much.

"Okay, buddy, let's get you into bed." I throw the covers open.

Payne stands by his books, his finger running along the spines. "Why can't we read the shark book?"

I inwardly cringe. We've been reading that same book for the past month. I'm not sure I can handle another reading, especially when I'm strung tighter than a piano wire.

"I'm bored with that book," I say. "Maybe we can go to the store tomorrow." I try to inject some excitement into my voice, hoping to sell him on the idea. "Just grab another book, sweetie." I pat his bed and widen my eyes.

"No." His fingers run along the spines of his books again and my head falls back in frustration.

"Come on, baby, let's read something else tonight and we'll go to the book store and see if we can find a different shark book tomorrow." I pat the bed again and he turns around, his lips turned down.

Mommy guilt rears its ugly head, but it's competing pretty hard with my needs right now. Thankfully, Payne cuts me a break.

"Promise?" he asks, sliding under the covers.

*Thank you*, I say internally to the heavens above.

"Yes, I promise. Now, get all comfy." My foot is tapping with impatience and I'm clenching my fists. I just want to get back downstairs.

I lean against the headboard with him and start reading. When we reach the second page, he places his hand down on the open book. "Mommy, too fast."

I smile down at him and nod. "Okay, I'll slow down."

I keep a good pace for a while, but it still feels like it's taking forever.

*Come on, Moon, just say good night, for fuck's sake.*

A century later, I finish and close the book.

"Mommy, why does the bunny say good night to everything?" Payne asks.

"Because that's what the book is about." I stand from the bed and tuck the covers under his chin.

"Maybe I should say good night to everything, too."

I kiss the top of his head and slide down the bed. "We can discuss that tomorrow."

"At Leo's store, they have puppies. Can we buy one?"

My hand pauses on the light switch. "We'll talk about it tomorrow morning, okay? Love you, Payne. Sweet dreams."

I turn off the light.

"Mommy?"

I release a breath and pause before I shut the door. "Yeah?"

"I really like Vance. Can he sleep over one night?"

I want to giggle but I stop myself. "We'll see. Good night."

I shut the door, thankful he doesn't stop me again.

Before I head back downstairs I make a quick stop in my bathroom to fluff my hair, apply a quick layer of face powder and brush my teeth. I blink my eyes to open them wider.

*I am not tired. I am not tired. I do not want to go to bed.*

Well, not alone anyway.

I force myself to walk at a normal pace down the stairs, even though anticipation has my legs wanting to sprint back to rejoin Vance.

"Trouble?" he asks, one arm across the back of the couch and a beer in his other hand. The television is tuned to the sports channel.

I can't help the way that my chest warms at seeing Vance so comfortable in my home—as if he belongs here.

"I opened you a bottle of white. That okay?" he asks as I round the coffee table to take a seat on the couch.

"Perfect. Thank you."

I sit there with my feet resting on my coffee table, watching the rundown of the day's sporting events that I care nothing about.

After a few minutes Vance leans forward, taking the wine glass from my hands and placing it on the table. "You into Oregon Ducks football?" he asks as he leans his weight on my body until my back is on the couch.

I glance at the TV screen which is showing some clips of a college football game. "Not at all." I shake my head.

"Good, because you're going to be my entertainment tonight." His lips descend and my body loses all the pent-up tension, relaxing into the soft cushions of my couch and melting into his body. His knee spreads my legs apart, and he fits himself between them.

"Vance?" I almost whisper.

"Yeah?" he murmurs as his tongue flicks at my earlobe.

"Can we go upstairs?" For some reason I can't stand the thought about having sex on the couch for our first time. I am not in high school.

He stands, holds out his hand. "I was hoping you'd say that, but I didn't want to assume."

I accept his offering and he pulls me up off the couch, then holds me steady at my hips.

"We don't have to sleep together," he says. "I'd be happy just to make out."

I fist his t-shirt in my hands. "I wouldn't." I pull him forward and he chuckles, letting me wield the power for a moment.

Once we reach the stairs, he lifts me up, throwing me over his shoulder and quietly walking up the stairs.

My bedroom is dark and I'm glad I took a few minutes this morning to tidy up my room and make my bed this morning. Not that I think that would deter either of us at this point. He shuts the door and flicks the lock.

"Just in case." We share a smile as I slide down his front until my feet reach to the floor.

"Remember when I was trying to tell you something earlier?" he asks, his two hands interlocked with mine.

I unhook one hand and place a finger over his lips. "Not now. I don't want to think about anything else tonight... just this."

"But..."

"No." I rise up on my tiptoes and place my lips to his, hoping he'll listen to me and kiss me back. I'm not usually a seize-the-moment person and I don't want this moment to pass me by because I began to retreat into my head with what if's.

He sucks my bottom lip into his mouth and my hands wrap around his neck, running through his soft, chestnut hair.

He pulls me flush against him and our lips touch, my eyes falling closed as we explore each other's mouth. Step by step, he guides us to the bed, his lips never leaving mine, where he lies on top of me. Half of his weight is pressed against me and it feels like heaven. His hands run down my sides, sneaking under the hem of my blouse and exploring my curves.

My nipples peak, ready to be played with. Just like the other night, his fingers pull down the cup of my bra to expose my breast, which fits perfectly in his palm. He massages my flesh, tweaking my nipple, and my head falls back to the mattress with a moan.

"You're so beautiful," he whispers, undoing the buttons on my shirt, slowly, like he's savouring every moment.

My blouse falls to the sides of my body and he runs his knuckles up and down the center of my stomach, spurring goose bumps to skitter along his path. His hand stops and I inhale a breath, waiting for him to undo my bra.

"Relax, Layla." He unclips the clasp between my breasts and bends down, kissing my skin while he brushes the fabric away so that my bra now lies with my blouse. "I knew you were perfect." He moves to my right breast, sucking it into his mouth, his tongue swirling the puckered tip around in his mouth like a cherry from a sundae.

"Far from perfect." My two hands run through his hair as he moves to my left breast, mimicking the same motion.

To say I'm self-conscious of my body would be a huge understatement. No one except Carver has seen me completely naked since I had children. Unlike Carver, I didn't sleep with anyone else after we got married, or since our separation.

I turned down a decent role last year that required a sex scene because I couldn't bring myself to do it. Then it dawns on me... what if Vance sees my body and decides I'm not a good fit for the movie?

I push him off me, sliding to the headboard, and crisscross each side of my blouse to cover myself.

"What's the matter?" Vance's alarmed face makes me cringe.

I'm all over the road here, giving him mixed signals. Who's to say he won't want to get off at the next available exit?

**15**

**Vance**

She's covering herself like I just groped her without her permission and with all the blood in my body heading south away from my brain it takes me a minute to try to catch up. "Layla?"

Her forehead falls to her knees and she mumbles something I can't understand.

"Do you want to look at me when you say that so I can understand what's happening here?"

She peeks one eye up and then rests her chin on her knees. "I'm not what you're used to... what you're expecting."

"What are you talking about?" Then it occurs to me. "Oh." I wave my hand up in the air. "Hey, we don't have to do anything. Am I pushing you too fast?"

Her shoulders lose all stiffness and she shakes her head. "No. That's not what I meant."

I run a hand through my hair. "You've lost me."

She blows out a stream of air and sits up on her knees, pulling her blouse open.

Damn, her tits are edible. Give me some chocolate sauce

and whip cream and let me lose a few hours playing with them kind of edible.

"See?" she says, in a tone that suggests I'm supposed to know where she's going with this.

"That you have great tits? Yeah, I know." I close my fists, resisting the urge to grab them. No way do I want to scare her.

"No." She glances down at herself and then back up to me. "The rest of me. See how imperfect I am?"

I lean back on my hands. I should have known. She's an actress and actresses are all perfectionists. "Layla, you're gorgeous." I say this in a tone that suggests she's off her rocker.

"No, the vision you had in your head before my clothes were off was gorgeous. See the stretch marks that Via left me with? They're always airbrushed out of the magazines if I happen to show my stomach. My C-section scar is hidden during a love scene on camera. I lost my perfect figure the minute I was pregnant with Payne. Now, you'll know you're getting a subpar-looking actress for your film and you'll want to cast someone else."

"Not true."

She ignores me, rushing to get off the bed and moving toward her bathroom. "But you know what? I'm fine with that," she continues on. "Maybe I should start applying for the mom roles. So what if I had my kids young and that ruins my chance of playing high-school parts even though I'm in my twenties? No Andrea Zuckerman for me."

Now I'm really confused. "Andrea Zuckerman?"

"You know, from *90210*? She was almost thirty playing a high-school junior. It's fine though, I'm fine with it. Because I think I do look pretty darn good for having two kids. You're right, my tits are great." She looks in the mirror outside her bathroom and places her hands on the bottom of her breasts, pushing them up. "With a little bit of tweaking they'll be good as new one day."

I walk up behind her, slowly, to not startle the crazy chick that has taken over Layla's brain at the moment. Sliding my hands under her arms, I cup her breasts with my hands, letting my thumbs run over her erect nipples.

"You're beautiful just the way you are. I wouldn't want to change anything about you. As far as the part, it's yours. You know that." I brush the loose strands of her hair away with my face and kiss her neck. "Don't ever be self-conscious around me because when I see you"—I purposely let my eyes meet hers in the mirror—"I always see perfection."

Her cheeks flush and it makes her even more beautiful.

"You're just saying that to get in my pants."

"Well, yeah, the raging hard-on I've had since we met is getting more and more distracting, but I'm not a liar. Also, I don't tend to get hard-ons from girls I don't find attractive."

Her head falls to my shoulder and I take the opportunity to devour her neck. Let her be a voyeur and witness first-hand in the mirror how much I want her with how I'm squeezing her tits in my hands and kissing her neck. Keeping one hand on her tit, I slide the other down, unfastening her jeans and pulling down her zipper. Digging my hand down the denim and under her lacy panties, I find her soaked, which elicits a growl from deep in my throat.

"Just relax." My lips travel the path of her neck, while my hand slowly eases the fabric off her body. "Watch me," I whisper and her eyes flutter open to stare at our reflection in the mirror.

Our eyes meet and the blouse drops to the floor, followed immediately by her bra, which leaves her only in her in jeans with a glimpse of her lacy red panties.

My hands move down either side of her waist, bypassing the small white lines, and I push her jeans down. Little by little she shimmies them down her legs and steps out of them, pushing them to the side on the floor.

"Look at you," I say. She stares back at me and then her gaze drops to her stomach. "How can you be blind to your beauty?"

With one more piece of thin fabric blocking the full view of her naked body, I hook my pointer fingers, push and slide the red lace down her thin legs.

Again, my lips travel a path from her shoulder up her neck and the light scent of her perfume lingers even after a long day.

"Look how mouth-watering you are." My hands explore the curves of her body. She's so much more than I ever imagined she'd be.

"Vance," she sighs, tilting her head further back, clearly enjoying what I'm doing.

"What do you want?" I cup one breast and massage her clit with my thumb.

"You. I just want you." She turns around in my arms and then grabs the hem of my t-shirt. "I think it's time for you to join this party."

I step back, teasing her with the hem of my t-shirt in my hands. "You want a *Magic Mike* show?" I chuckle, but she grabs a fistful of my shirt and pulls me toward the bed.

"Nah, we'll save that for later. I've wanted to strip you down for some time."

I stand there with my back to the mattress. "I had something similar on my wish list."

She shakes her head, unbuckling my jeans. "Well, I'll be sure to get the full list later so I can check all the boxes."

My jeans drop seconds later and she's quick to shed my boxer briefs right after. On her way back up my body, her hands glide along my sides, bringing the t-shirt up my chest as she goes. Since I'm a helpful kind of guy, I raise my hands and toss it over my head to join my pile of clothes on the floor.

"Now we're both ready for some fun."

I pick her up and throw her down the bed. She yelps and I cover her mouth with my hand so she won't wake the kids.

Leaning down on the bed, I remove my hand and cover it with my mouth, allowing our tongues to savor the taste of each other. Her hands move to the back of my head, her short nails running along my hair. Our movements are slow and deliberate, searching for the area of each other's body that will drive the other to the brink.

For Layla, it's the tiniest spot right under her ear. She arches her back when I push her hair off her neck and sprinkle the lightest of kisses there. Goose bumps break out across her silky skin when my knuckles run down her stomach. Her soft moans and deep breaths turn her into a goddess sprawled out on top of her pink sheets. I'm not sure I could ever get my fill of exploring her body. I'm already addicted to finding every inch of exposed flesh that makes her squirm beneath me.

We're so lost in each other that I fail to realize the position we're in. I'm on top of her, my cock poised at her slick entrance. Her arms are stretched around me now, her hands on my ass, pushing me toward her. I use my knees to open her legs further.

I push up and ask, "Condom?" praying I don't need to dig into my jeans on the floor because that would mean separating our bodies.

"Drawer on the right," she pants out, looking up at me with heavy-lidded eyes.

I smile. Perfect. I only have to shift my weight but can stay between her legs and her hands can continue to knead my flesh.

I find one loose condom in the drawer and sit up on my knees in front of her.

She runs her hands up and down my torso while I rip the foil packet open. I'm sure I set a new record for myself in the wrapper-to-dick race. When I lean back over her, her hands find their place on the back of my neck.

The heat between her legs is like a priceless piece of art, coaxing me closer with its beauty as I slip into her slickness. Fuck, she feels like heaven. Again, I move my knees to widen her legs, wanting to be as deep inside her as possible.

"Oh, my God." Layla's head falls off the edge of the bed and her legs wrap around my waist.

The contraction of her thighs on my waist while I thrust in and out of her becomes unbearable—in the best way.

"Whatever you're doing with the legs, keep it up. You're driving me insane."

She smiles up at me and the pig in me can't help but admire the way her tits bounce up and down as I drive into her. How could this woman not know how beautiful she is?

Her pussy and my dick are like some damn pulley system, moving with a smoothness I've never encountered. You'd think we'd mastered this sex thing with each other through a long relationship, but this is our first time. There should be some sort of awkwardness as we work to discover one another's bodies, but our sex is fucking perfect. Like a scene from a movie that looks spectacular, without the fifty takes to get there.

"Look at me, Vance," she whispers. "Be in the moment."

I glance down, realizing I'm so busy psychoanalyzing our relationship that I'm missing the best part—watching her get off. Staring into her eyes, eyes that are now glossed over with heavy lids, I grind small circles into her.

Her fingers tighten, and for the first time I wish I had long hair for her to pull. She rises and her lips crash to mine.

Caging her head in between my arms, I kiss her while I grind in and out of her slick heat. I brush away the hair on her forehead and savor the last moments before we both fall into ecstasy.

Her own grinding quickens and I match her pace, pulling my mouth from hers. She grips the sheets in her hands but she keeps her legs wrapped around me while I push her body to the limit, sending her tumbling over that cliff and straight into undiluted pleasure. She moans and tries to keep her eyes open, but fails and she bucks underneath me, her thighs squeezing me tight. Eventually, she comes down from her high, her body losing the stiffness, the sheets finally free from her grip.

I come seconds later, my sweaty body falling onto hers.

Jesus, I can't wait until we can do that again.

## 16

### Vance

Someone is banging on the door.

"Fucking Jagger." I roll back over, grabbing my free pillow and covering my head.

"Hello, that's my pillow," a soft voice says and then soft fingers touch my stomach. "We have a problem."

I whip the pillow off my head and turn over.

Layla. Yes. Layla. We fucked four times last night. Everything rushes to the forefront of my mind and I sit up, the sheet twisting around my leg.

I stare at the door and Layla giggles.

"Mommy!" Payne screams on the other side of the door.

"Ma?" a sweet voice says *from inside the room* and I jump out of the bed. The twisted sheet around my leg catches me and I fall buck ass naked head first to the hardwood floor.

Layla's laughing so hard when she peers over the edge of the bed that her entire face is lit up like the Rockefeller tree at Christmas.

"Where's Via?" I ask, taking in every inch of the room and not seeing her.

She holds up a video monitor and wiggles it side to side. There's Via, standing up in her crib.

"I should have left." I finally free myself from the sheet and stand up.

Layla's gaze rakes up and down my naked body.

"I'm glad you enjoy what you see, but what are we going to do?" I whisper-shout.

"Mommy!" Payne tries the doorknob and I hurriedly grab my jeans.

"Well, we can't let Payne see you. He'll be upset he missed the sleepover." She giggles again. Now I see what makes Layla giddy—orgasms. Six to be exact.

I toss my t-shirt over my head.

"You go hide in the bathroom. I'll grab my robe and get him and Via downstairs. You can sneak out the front door."

She rises from the bed and walks as fast as she can to the bathroom. A minute later she comes out with a silk robe wrapped around her mouthwatering body.

"Hey," I say, pulling her toward me with the tie of the robe.

"Mommy!" Payne bangs on the door.

"Just one second, honey," Layla says and he stops his pounding. "Go downstairs and turn on the television, I'll be down in a second with Via."

"Okay."

We both wait until we can no longer hear his footsteps walking down the hall.

I slide my hands through the robe, spreading the silky fabric in the front wide and bringing her naked front to my body. "I really enjoyed last night."

"Me, too."

I kiss her forehead. "What are you doing tonight?"

Her eyebrows scrunch and she puts on her best thinking

hard expression. "I don't have anything. I have shooting first thing tomorrow."

"Oh." My head falls forward so that our foreheads meet. "My last week as the manny."

She pushes up on her tiptoes and places a sweet kiss on my lips. "You can play manny anytime you want."

A wail of a cry rings out from the video monitor. To make matters worse, Payne's stomping footsteps up the stairs can probably be heard in the house next door.

"One, two," I say.

*Bang. Bang.*

"Mommy, the TV doesn't work."

"Okay, give me a second." Layla's head falls to my shoulder.

"I wish I could help you this morning, but I feel like a teenage boy who's about to be caught by his girlfriend's dad after he felt her up on the couch in the basement."

She muffles her giggle into my shoulder. "Nah." She stands straight. "It's better this way."

I place my hands on either side of her face and kiss her, hoping like hell it conveys how much I'm going to miss her company today.

"Talk to you later?" I ask when I pull away.

"Of course. Thanks for a great night." She heads toward the door and I walk toward the bathroom.

"Ditto," I say and sneak through the door, shutting it behind me.

A second later I hear Layla talking to Payne and through the monitor, I hear her talking to Via as she changes her diaper and her clothes before taking her downstairs.

I stand there listening to their morning routine and think about what a great mother she is and how until her, I didn't know how attractive a quality it would be.

———

I GOTTA GIVE it to Layla, she's good at stealth maneuvers. She had the kids in the kitchen eating breakfast in record time as I shot down the stairs and out the front door as quickly and as quietly as I could.

It wasn't until I reached the car that I realized something was off.

I've slept with my fair share of girls, most of whom I didn't do the sleepover thing with. But the odd time I did spend the night, it was like I had poison oak from the way my body itched around them until the time that I was safe and secure in my car. With Layla though, it's different. I *want* to be back in that house. I *want* to be making pancakes with her for the kids. I *want* to sit on the couch and read the paper, drinking coffee, and feasting my greedy gaze on her whenever I want.

What the hell is happening to me? I'm not good with kids. I'm not a family man. I'll only end up hurting them all, and after what Carver did—Layla hasn't said much on that front, but I'm not an idiot, I can read between the lines (and, okay, the gossip mags)—they don't need me adding gasoline to their lives.

Regardless of the speech I'm giving myself, my car has a mind of its own and heads north when it should go south and a few minutes later I find myself in front of the donut place. Even worse, I walk in and order a dozen donuts, two coffees, and two chocolate milks. Then somehow, I end up outside Layla's house again.

Walking up the walkway, I realize that I have no fucking idea what I'm doing. I *have* to tell Layla how I sabotaged her career.

But when Layla opens the door with that robe on and a spatula in her hands with a confused expression on her face, I realize the truth—I'm too scared. This woman and her children have come to mean too much to me to risk it. I've sabotaged a lot of things in my life, but this, whatever this is between us, I refuse to ruin.

"Hey," she says, the softest smile gracing her lips.

"Breakfast?" I ask, holding up the donuts.

"You didn't." She shakes her head and I bend down, kissing her to quiet her.

"I wanted to." Then I slide past her and head toward the kitchen where I get the best thank you from both kids when they attach themselves onto my legs.

Who needs to be a rock star? These kids treat me like I'm Pablo from the Backyardigans—who up until a couple of weeks ago I would have had no idea existed.

———

"YOU'RE FUCKING this entire thing up." Jagger slams the magazine down on the table.

The magazine with a picture of me at Layla's front door with donuts and coffee. We should be thankful they didn't catch me leaving fifteen minutes before that.

"You should be glad they haven't figured out who you are yet. I say yet, because they will." He flips his tie back over his shoulder, dousing his pancakes with syrup. "Not to mention, when is this whole manny shit over? I need your undivided attention on getting this movie off the ground."

Jagger glances over his shoulder to Payne, who's playing the claw game again, just like he was the time he and Layla were here.

"Lower your voice. This is my last week." I cut up Payne's blueberry pancakes and ask the waitress to refill his chocolate milk.

"Aren't you a regular Alice from *The Brady Bunch*."

I roll my eyes because he's probably never even watched one episode of that show, it's so old.

"What about that one?" He nods to Via in the high chair.

She had a stomach bug yesterday so I told Layla I'd watch her today, too.

"Why don't you stop acting like"—I cover Via's ears and she squirms—"an asshole."

"What are you, Vince Vaughn with the earmuffs thing? I shut up when you made this deal because I thought, man, he's really going balls to the wall to get this script made. But now —" His manicured nail points to the magazine again. The title still puts bile in my throat.

*Watch Out, Carver, There's A New Daddy On Duty.*

"You're being called daddy and about to get down on bended knee, according to the press. Let's remember"—he leans forward and lowers his voice—"you had her fired from what was her best opportunity to catapult her career after she was too old to be the star over at the network that shall not be named that starts with a D." He shakes his head while he chews. "This whole thing is going to blow up in your face," he says, pointing his fork in my direction.

I roll my eyes and push my hands down on the table so I can lean in, only inches away from him.

"I'm warning you now, stop making me feel guilty. I made a mistake."

His hands fly up in the air. "You've fallen for her." He points his fork my way again and this time Via reaches out to grab it, but Jagger moves it out of her reach. "I can't even stop you anymore, you've been branded by her."

"I have not been branded, but yes"—I check to make sure Payne is busy—"I have fallen for her. She's amazing."

"Cue glistening eyes and heart pupils." Jagger buries his head into his meal, his fork scratching along the plate.

"Uncle Jagger is angry," I say to Via, who is too busy making her eggs and ketchup into a masterpiece to care.

"Now you're talking baby talk?" He shakes his head, sipping his coffee.

"What did I miss?" Leo slides in next to Jagger.

After shifting closer to the wall, Jagger takes another bite of his pancake before speaking. "Just that Vance is a pussy who can't keep his dick in his pants." Jagger's voice is on that edge between annoyed and joking, but I'm pretty sure he's venturing into more annoyed territory right now.

"Whoa." Leo moves to cover Via's ears. "Innocent ears, man."

I raise my eyebrows.

Jagger rolls his eyes. "Where are my boys? You've both turned so domesticated."

The waitress comes over, pen and paper poised over her pad, and looks to Leo.

"Just coffee, in a to-go. I gotta run."

"Run? You aren't going to eat?" I ask because I'd like him to be a buffer between Jagger and me.

"No, I gotta do an Instagram live thing at the shop."

"What?" Jagger mumbles with a full mouth, cocking an eyebrow at Leo.

Leo picks up a fork and stabs a three-stack of cut-up pancakes off Jagger's plate. "Marketing, man."

Jagger slides his plate away from Leo. "You need a PR person."

Leo swallows down the pancakes. "No way. I'm not giving up control to some millennial who's going to tell me I need to connect more with my audience, appeal to my ideal consumer, blah, blah, blah."

"You're insane. Your business will suffer if you don't hand over some responsibility soon. You're growing way too fast."

See why I wanted Leo to stick around? Jagger's moved on to fixing Leo's life now. Jagger is, and always will be, a fixer.

The waitress returns with Leo's coffee and a second later he's standing with his to-go cup in his hand.

"Duggie?" Via reaches out to Leo with a ketchup-covered hand, marking his pants.

"Shit," he says, examining the damage. Then he bends down to Via and makes a funny face at her while he says, "You're one lucky girl it was me and not him." He points to Jagger.

Via giggles.

Leo points outside. "Doggie is outside and needs to get to work." He winks and then waves at us out the door.

"He's a moron," Jagger says, taking another sip of his coffee.

I shake my head. "You're so opinionated. Why don't you let us all live our lives?" I ask. "Payne," I call him over.

"Because you're bound to screw it up. Mark my words, this situation you've gotten yourself in is trouble." Jagger pushes his plate away, wiping his mouth with the napkin and throwing the balled-up paper on his plate.

"You have no idea what the future holds."

"Allow me to go Oprah on your ass for a second because here's what I know for sure—this is L.A., she's an actress with one marriage under her belt. You're an aspiring scriptwriter who needs to concentrate on his career for a while and not worry about dipping his writer's pen in the fountain of youth. This shit is highly combustible material and you're dancing around all over the place with a lit match. Do I like what's going on? No, I don't, not because I don't want you to have a wife or a kid, but because I'm a dream-maker. That's what I do for my clients. I make their dreams come true." He slides out of the booth, grabbing cash from inside his suit jacket, tossing it on the table. "Enjoy playing house, but if the tabloids find out who you are, she's going to be pissed and you can forget her doing the film, which means we'll be back to square one searching for a new investor."

"Jagger, I plan on telling her."

His entire body stiffens. "No. You have to keep it quiet at this point."

"I can't. She has to know the truth."

I'll admit, I've waffled myself about coming clean, but the reality is that if I want Layla and I to stand a real chance of lasting I have to tell her the truth.

He blows out a breath, stuffs his hands in the pockets of his slacks, rolling back on his heels. "Do me a favor. We're flying out to Chicago to meet the investor in two weeks. Just give me until then. Maybe if Hannah loves that boyish grin of yours she'll still invest after Layla tells you to go fuck yourself."

"Jagger." I nod to Via.

"She's playing with her eggs and ketchup, she doesn't even understand what we're saying."

Payne runs over, finally growing bored of the game and willing to eat his breakfast.

"See you, buddy." Jagger holds out his fist for a bump.

Payne stares at it and then me and limply fist-bumps him. Guess Jagger Kale doesn't win everyone over.

"Remember what I said, Vance. Two weeks." Jagger makes a motion to seal his lips and throw the key away.

I roll my eyes. Dork. "Say bye to Jagger."

Payne says, "Bye," and Via waves her soiled hand toward him.

"See you, Manny dearest."

Then it's just the three of us left, so I take a selfie of us all and send Layla the picture, taking a moment to stare at the screen and think of how much I'd miss these two if Jagger's right and this all goes to shit because I've been an idiot.

## 17

## Layla

"Something smells yummy." I shut the front door, take off my jacket and place my bag on the floor of the foyer.

Redoing a scene today where I'm stuck in the back of the smallest car ever has left my back aching. On the way to the kitchen to find out what's baking, I stop to try to crack my back a few times.

A smile graces my lips the minute I step into the sweet-smelling space. There's flour on the floor, sugar in Vance's hair, a broken egg on the counter.

"Is there actually something baking, or did you just spread everything around?"

Vance turns from the oven, and I'm sucker-punched by the magnitude of his smile, as if he's waited all day to see me. He points to the hallway and glances to the family room. There are the kids, Payne on his stomach watching a cartoon and Via lost in her bucket of toys.

I backstep out of the room, but not as fast as Vance approaches me. My back hits the solid wall of his chest and he spins me to face him, his fingers looping through the belt loops of my jeans, and he smashes his lips to mine. It doesn't take long for our mouths to find our rhythm, our tongues teasing and dancing with each other. I grip his strong shoulders, keeping him exactly where he's standing.

The kiss ends and he rests his forehead on mine. "I missed you."

It's almost as if I can feel the pang of Cupid's arrow, searing me to this man. I'm not sure Carver ever told me he missed me—ever. And we'd been separated for months at a time depending on where and what we were filming.

"You did?"

He draws back, tilting his head in a questioning way. I smack his chest and he chuckles. "When will you stop doubting my attraction to you?" His arms pull me into a hug, his lips finding his favorite spot—or maybe mine—to kiss my neck.

"It's not that. I can feel your attraction pressing into my stomach right now. I'm just surprised. You seem to have gone from fun flirting to putting a ring on it." I raise my hand. "Not that I'm looking for a ring," I add.

"You're right."

"I am?" Now it's my head drawing back.

"Yeah." He shrugs one shoulder and my eyes zero in on his biceps. Another tight t-shirt covering it up. "Are you a witch?" He leans forward, his eyes glimmering with mirth as they stare into mine. "Did you sneak some kind of potion into my drink? I mean it couldn't possibly be because you're beautiful, or because you're funny, or you know what?" He raises his finger in the air. "My mom always said to stick with a woman who can cook and clean." He takes his finger and runs it along the edge of the table. "I guess one out of two isn't bad, right?"

I smack his stomach and he chuckles, linking his hand with mine and pulling me further into the kitchen.

"So, what did you bake?" I ask, sitting down on the breakfast stool and swiping some sugar off the counter.

Vance concentrates on my finger as I lick the sugar off. Once I realize he's staring, I place it in my mouth and suck it off.

"Well, Payne said you love sugar cookies." He takes a couple of steps to the side and glances into the family room. "He lasted until the eggs," he whispers.

I chuckle. "Sounds about right."

He wipes down the counter. "Bad part is I have no dinner because I guess I'm not the baker I thought I was."

"You thought you were a baker?" My eyes find the sink full of discarded bowls and spoons and I stifle a laugh.

"My mom had a rule during the holidays. Everyone does something. I always did desserts with my sister. I guess I never realized she did the majority of the work." His lips tip up at the corner in that 'I kind of really knew that though' way.

"I bet your sister has a lot of stories about you."

He pours me a glass of wine and places it in front of me. "It'll be a long time before you meet Charlie."

"Charlie's your sister?"

He twists open his beer bottle with his shirt, granting me a sneak peek of that taut stomach that sends a thrill straight to my girly parts.

"Charlotte, actually, but the entire town calls her Charlie. She recently just hooked up with my best friend from high school."

My eyes widen. "You allowed that?"

He chuckles, his head falling back. "You'll understand how I have zero control over what she does or doesn't do when you meet my sister."

The fact he's implying that I will one day meet her calms the nerves that have been running like a freight train through my veins lately. I mean, is Vance really different than every other man in this town? He feels different, but this city sells fantasy for a living.

"Plus"—he rolls his eyes—"she's loved him since she was a kid, so I kinda think she deserves him and I couldn't have handpicked a better guy for her. They're expecting their first child together and I'm telling you... I couldn't be more excited to be an uncle."

I sip my wine, admiring the way he talks about his family. There's a warmth in his voice that seems to be reserved only for them. Carver hated his and never even invited them to the baptism for either Payne or Via. I'm not a huge fan of mine since they siphoned money away from me when I was a kid, but I tolerate them. At times they were all I had.

"Tell me about your town," I say, not wanting him to stop, wanting to know anything and everything about this man.

He leans against the counter, staring off toward the fridge. "It's a small town in Oregon. One where everyone knows everyone's business, but it's also the kindest town with the best people. Yeah, it can take you about an hour to run an errand because of how many people you have to stop and chat up, but everyone wants the best for everyone. There's fundraisers when someone has a hardship, a Christmas parade and a tree-lighting ceremony everyone attends. Sometimes I think I'll end up back there if I visit too much, so I keep my distance."

"Makes me wonder why you ever left."

A soft laugh comes from his closed mouth. When he talks to his feet, his lips tip down for the first time in our conversation. "I wanted more. I wanted to be part of the rich and famous lifestyle, wanted to be the superstar." He shrugs.

"How many scripts have you sold?"

He raises his head and inhales a deep breath. "This is my first." His voice is so low I can barely hear him.

"Then what have you been doing? Did you come down here to act originally?" I sip my wine, wondering if I'm prying too much, but he's been so open tonight and I figure he'll tell me if I am.

"No, I wanted to be a scriptwriter since I moved to L.A. a decade ago. My first one was horrible and I kept getting rejections. Eventually all the money I had saved up was gone and I had to find a job." He downs a big gulp of beer. "I took a job as an assistant to an assistant of a producer. Over the years, I climbed my way up."

"Long hours, I bet."

He huffs. "Yeah, but then last year I realized I hadn't been happy for a while and decided it was time to finally do what I set out to do. Try to make the dream happen."

I smile. "That's awesome. That takes a lot of guts." I lean across the counter. "Makes me want to act even better for your film so it's a success." I laugh so he knows I'm totally joking.

He nods. "I still wonder if it's actually going to happen. I'll believe it when I'm walking down that red carpet."

I place my hand on his forearm. "It will happen and it's going to be a great success. I have intuition on these things."

"Unless you're psychic, I'll be one breath from an anxiety attack until then." He chugs the rest of his beer and the bottle clinks onto my granite countertop.

"So, what did you produce? Anything I'd know?"

The buzzer goes off for the cookies and Payne runs into the kitchen.

"Hi, Mommy!" He gives me a quick hug and then looks at Vance. "Are they ready?" He's jumping up and down, excitement brimming out of him.

"Hold on, let me get them out." Vance takes the tray out and the circular sugar cookies look lightly browned and the perfect amount of crisp.

"I'd say you do that pretty well."

Vance shares a heated look with me before returning his attention to the baking tray. Via toddles in, so I pick her up before she latches onto Vance's leg.

"I'm crossing fingers they taste as good as they look." He catches my eyes above Payne's head and I so want to kiss him right now, but I know I can't do that to the kids just yet. We need more time before the kids think anything is going on with us.

"Can I have one?" Payne asks, his fingers already moving to the hot sheet.

"Let them cool for at least a couple of minutes," Vance says and then his gaze veers over to me again. "And you have to ask your mom." He winks.

"Make me the bad guy, huh?" I move Via's hands away from reaching out. "One each and then dinner."

"Yay!" Payne runs around in circles. Via takes the cue from her brother and follows suit, screaming her excitement even though she doesn't know what's going on.

"How about we order pizza for dinner?" Vance asks, pulling his phone out.

"You do realize you're going to have to write in that your female lead is ten pounds heavier pretty soon, right?" I place Via in her high chair and glance over my shoulder at him.

Vance's eyes are focused on my ass. "You have no problem there."

A supercharged current concentrates itself between my legs. If my kids weren't here, I think I'd crawl up on the counter and have him eat me rather than the cookies.

———

VANCE SHUTS Payne's door quietly behind him. I'll admit my feelings were a tad hurt when Payne asked for Vance to read him his story tonight instead of me. Even with my heart soaring seeing the two of them side by side on Payne's bed reading about dinosaurs, I kind of wish there was room for three.

Via's been fast asleep since right after dinner so I check on her and then shut the door, leaving us alone in the hallway.

"I have to frost the cookies," Vance says, dodging me in my bedroom doorway and heading down the stairs.

"Seriously?" I ask, flabbergasted that the man who's been eyeing my tits and ass all night just passed up on the promise of seeing them in all their glory to... frost cookies.

"I promised Payne I'd do it," he tosses out over his shoulder before heading down the stairs.

Reluctantly, I follow. "Vance." I stand in the doorway to the kitchen where he's pulling out a stainless-steel bowl.

He looks up at me. "Don't worry, babe, I plan on sugaring your cookie tonight, too." He winks.

I push off the wall and decide I might as well help him to get it done faster. "Do you know how to make icing?" I ask, watching him dump a bunch of powdered sugar into a bowl.

"Not really, but I looked up a recipe online."

"Okay, pull out your phone."

"I looked at it earlier. I think I can wing it."

I cock an eyebrow. Not that I'm a better option. Other than playing a baker's assistant for a made-for-TV movie once, I know nothing about baking. "Interesting. Do you wing everything you do?"

He pours the milk in without measuring. "Pretty sure you enjoy it when I wing it." He knocks his shoulder to mine and places his lips out for me, requesting a kiss.

I grant his wish, planting a short kiss to his lips, and then he pours some vanilla into the bowl. It's anyone's guess as to how much.

"I'm pretty sure baking isn't like cooking. You need to measure." I hoist myself up on the counter.

Grabbing the hand mixer, he starts beating the ingredients together. Ingredients I didn't even know I had. I have to assume my mom bought them when she made Christmas pies here last month.

"Trust me," he says, and even though I know he's just talking about the cookies, I find that I do—on an even deeper level.

His attention is fixed on the bowl and I have to say his concoction looks good, except it's a little watery. He dumps more powdered sugar in and then grabs some corn syrup and pours it in.

"You're seriously going to make me have to use the excuse that cameras make you gain twenty pounds, not ten." I pick up the bottom. "Pure sugar."

The mixer stops and he swipes up a glob with his finger. He holds his finger in front of my mouth.

"Stop worrying about your figure. You could gain a few pounds and it wouldn't affect your part." He inches his finger closer.

I slowly stick my tongue out and curl it around the end of his finger, rimming the tip and enjoying the way his eyelids hood and his breath labors while my teeth scrape along the underside of his finger. Encasing my mouth over his entire finger, I suck off the icing, twirling my tongue around his finger while my eyes lock with his.

Once I let his finger go with a pop, his hands move to my ass and he slides me forward on the counter.

"Temptress." His lips meet mine and our mouths collide in a fury, all our pent-up adrenaline of wanting each other all night finally finding an outlet.

His mouth moves off mine, but his hands grab the hem of my shirt and tear it from my body. His frantic motions continue as he unhooks my bra, letting it fall and eventually landing on the floor. He squeezes them a little more than is comfortable, but it's exactly what I need.

"I've been half hard all day remembering you naked under me last night." Without me saying anything, his hand slides up my legs under my skirt. "When you walked in with that skirt on I had to shift my stance."

With every confession, my body grows hotter, my pussy wetter.

He motions for me to lift up a bit and he slides my pants to my ankles and I give a couple of kicks until they, too, fall to the floor.

He uses one finger to brush along the outside of my panties and my body loses all tension until I feel about the same consistency as the icing in the bowl beside me.

"God," I sigh, my head falling back.

With one hand on my tit and the other on the outside lace of my panties, he teases me with his expert movements.

I want him. All of him. All of the time.

I've been starved of this kind of attention my entire life and I didn't even know it until this man entered it. He's turned me upside down. Nothing in my past compares to how he makes me feel. I thought I had an okay love life. I mean, Carver loved me. I know he did in his own way. But Vance, he's like a bear outside a cabin, willing to claw his way through to me as though he's going to explode if he can't have me. As animalistic as that sounds, I love how much he wants me.

His finger slides between my pussy and my panties and his mouth opens slightly in awe.

"You like?" I ask.

Taking that half-hour lunch to get a wax job seems well worth listening to my stomach grumbling all afternoon.

"Fuck, yeah," he growls.

He grabs my panties and tears them. Literally tears them from my body and tosses them on the floor.

"I don't want anything in my way." His lips find my neck and his nibbles turn to light bites.

"Those were new." I don't really care, I just like our push and pull.

"I'll replace them. You can model new ones for me."

See, this is what I'm talking about. He's perfection.

His hand moves to cover my entire mound. His finger slides along my wetness. "I need to taste you."

Gently pushing me so my back lies on the counter, he falls to his knees in front of me.

One flick of the tongue is all it takes for me to be on the edge of an orgasm. I knew waxing was going to make me more sensitive, but damn, I need to try to think of something other than his mouth on me so I can make this last.

"Shit," I mumble, struggling for breath as he sucks my nub into his mouth. "Who taught you this? Because I'd like to give them an award."

His laugh is muffled by my pussy and I thread my fingers through his hair to keep him in place.

He licks up and down, he sucks, he twirls his tongue and by the time I'm a screaming, writhing mess, a deep rumbling laugh comes from him and he leans back.

"Shit, I think you're going to make me bald." His hand instinctively moves to his scalp.

"Let me make it up to you," I practically purr.

"What did you have in mind?" he asks in a husky voice.

"Why don't you take your pants off and I'll show you." I arch a brow, daring him to do so.

I focus on him unbuttoning his jeans and then they fall to the floor. A second later he pulls his boxer briefs down and kicks them to the side.

He stands there in all his perfection and my mouth

waters. I want so badly to taste him. I lick my lips and Vance's eyes track every movement.

"I'm clean," he says.

Music to my ears. I don't respond, simply grin at him for a minute before spinning myself on the counter so my back is to him. Then I slowly ease myself back. I'm now sprawled across the counter, my head dangling off the end, upside down in front of Vance.

"Fuck," he says and pushes a hand through his hair.

I reach out and grab the base of his hard length, directing him toward me. I open my mouth wide and it doesn't take much encouragement before Vance is pushing himself to the back of my throat.

"Jesus," he pants out.

I'll be honest—I've never actually given head this way, but I've seen it in porn and since the opportunity presented itself, I figured why the hell not?

He braces his hands on the edge of the counter and pushes all the way in to the base, his eyes rolling back in his head when he breaches the back of my throat.

It's surprisingly easy to do in this position and I moan as I imagine what we must look like. Vance must feel the vibrations of the sound on his cock because he groans and slides himself out between my lips and immediately pushes his shaft back in, a little harder this time.

I use my hand to cup his balls while he thrusts into my mouth. I manage to keep my throat relaxed as I watch him gaze intently down at where my lips are wrapped around his cock. When he leans forward and starts playing with my nub I'm almost as lost in the building pleasure as he is.

Without warning he pulls himself from my mouth and takes a step back. When I've righted myself and am sitting on top of the counter again, I give him a questioning gaze.

He's stroking himself and studying my very naked body.

"That was fucking hot, but if we go any longer I'm not going to last. I've got plans for that pussy and they involve my cock being inside it for a while."

I grin. "I have an IUD," I say, wanting nothing between us.

"Perfect."

He winks, picks me up and deposits me on the kitchen table. He controls every move from how far apart my legs are to exactly where he wants my ass at the edge.

When he pushes inside me, my stomach contracts from the sheer pleasure of the feel of me stretching around him. I want him to delve deeper. I want him to push harder. I want to feel every pent-up emotion of want grow inside of him.

There's no slow and romantic rhythm this time around. The way he takes me is hard and uncontrolled and fierce. The crumbs from dinner itch underneath my back, but I don't care. I don't focus on that. I can't when I see the expression of need and ownership on his face. He's biting his bottom lip and he's staring down between my legs at where he's entering me.

After a minute, his gaze shifts to my tits and lastly my eyes. "I could fuck you for the rest of my life."

He continues his assault on my body, moving in and out of me at a rapid-fire pace and circling his hips. I grip the edge of the kitchen table to keep from sliding back. His fingertips dig into my thighs and though it's a little painful it makes me even hotter for him. So much so that the second he places his thumb on my engorged clit I go off. I cry out and buck up underneath him and in the midst of this Vance pulls out, jerks himself a few times and his hot cum coats the top of my pussy.

"Mommy?"

We both freeze, wide-eyed.

"Payne, it's time for bed." I inhale a deep breath.

"I heard noises. What are you guys doing?"

The one good thing is I know he's upstairs since I put the baby gate across when I came down.

I shoot Vance a 'help me out here' look.

"Go to bed, buddy, I'm just sugaring the cookies," he says.

I press my lips together to try to keep from laughing, but Vance covers my mouth and I shake my head at his innuendo.

"Oh, yay!" Payne says.

"Get to bed so you can have one tomorrow," Vance continues, a smile teasing at his lips.

"I'm going," he says.

We hear the door shut and Vance lets go of my mouth.

"You're bad," I say, but he leans forward and kisses me.

"Please, you love me sugaring the cookie as much as I do." He winks. "Now let's get you cleaned up."

**18**

## Vance

"Put your fucking phone down. This is a guys' trip." Jagger tries to snatch my phone from my hands, but I dodge his attempts.

"We aren't twenty-one, shithead." I finish my text to Layla.

**Me:** *Miss you already.*

I'm waiting for the three dots to appear when the flight attendant places a vodka tonic on my tray. I glance to the side at Jagger, who raises his own drink in the air. Shifting my eyes to Leo, I see him raising his beer.

My phone dings and Leo smiles, shaking his head because he already knows the shit Jagger is going to give me.

I glance down at my phone to find a picture of Layla, Via, and Payne—all with frowns on their faces. A second later and my phone dings again.

**Layla:** *Have fun and good luck with the investor. We'll miss you. See you when you get home.* 

**Me:** *Thank you. I'll text you when we land.*

The pilot comes over the speaker and asks everyone to turn their electronics to airplane mode.

"Finally," Jagger says across the aisle.

"I'm not sure why you have such a problem with Layla."

I've dealt with the jokes, the heavy sighs, and his predictions that we won't make it. We're going to hash this out now.

"Layla isn't the problem. You know the problem. You shouldn't be dating the actress who's going to star in your film."

"Let it go. I'm a big boy."

"Yeah, Jagger, it's really none of your business," Leo chimes in and I fistbump him. "Our Vancey is all grown up with a girlfriend. Deal with it." Leo grabs my shoulder, rocking me a few times to the side.

Jagger closes his eyes once the pilot says we're ready for take-off and that ends the conversation. Thank God, he's afraid to fly or I'd probably have to listen to him the entire ride.

During the flight, Leo and Jagger both hammer away on their computers, Leo with headphones on and Jagger working on his third drink, me with my script on the table. I flip through the pages, looking at the rewrites that the script manager I hired is suggesting. She seems to be on the same side as Layla—that the romance is missing and I have to redo the majority of the intimate scenes to show that side of the hero.

Midflight, Leo nudges me. "Hey, I think what's happening with Layla is awesome." He runs his hand through his dark blond hair and then inches forward to check out Jagger.

I follow his movements to see Jagger is passed out cold. Probably from his four drinks. The man hates to fly, so it's probably better he's asleep. I won't even tell you about the time we went to St. Croix and we had to drug him just to get him on the plane. Oops, I guess I just did. Payback's a bitch, friend.

"Thanks." It's nice one of my friends can be happy for me.

"You guys moved fast, huh?"

I thought he said he was just happy for me? Noticing my confused expression, he quickly raises his hands.

"I'm not saying it's bad, I'm just curious how you guys started going Mach nine."

I sip my water and focus on the sound of the ice jiggling in the glass for a moment. "I'm not sure either. One minute I just wanted to kiss her and the next thing I know I want to spend every second with her."

He nods like he understands what I'm saying. "I wish you guys luck. What's up with the ex? Carver Sterling, right?"

I shake my head. Asshole. "Not much. I guess he's filming, but he's called a total of two times since I've been around."

"He has to know you're in the picture, what with the photos of you surfacing."

Technically, no paps have been able to see my face yet. But it sucks sneaking through back doors and taking Ubers and taxis all the time. Not to mention, we can't go anywhere public.

"I've been able to dodge them, but after I meet the investor and charm her to love me, I'm telling Layla. I gave Jagger my word that I'd wait until after this meeting and after everything he's done for me I don't want to screw him over. But I can't keep the secret anymore. I need it over and done with so we can move forward."

"I'm sure she's not going to care. I mean, it's one part. She'll know what you guys have."

I sip my drink. I pray he's right because the guilt gnaws at me.

"Enough about me though. I wanna know why you're not dating anyone." I push my own issues away because there's not much more to be done at this point except get this meeting with the investor over and done with and then man up and tell Layla. The more I think about it, the more I just want to shoot her a text, but that's not the right way to tell her.

Leo presses his lips together for a second before answering. "I hate the L.A. dating scene. Everyone wants to be something they're not, there's zero loyalty, and most women here are so wrapped up in what they look like, they don't bother looking past the surface to work on what's inside. Besides, actresses are a handful and after that clinger Yvette I decided to concentrate on the business for a while."

"You're happy though?" I ask, because I'm a firm believer friends don't ask friends enough. Especially guys. Hell, I barely asked my best buddy from high school if he was all right after he lost his wife once the funeral had passed. I tried to be there for him, but I didn't ask how he was feeling about the situation. It was obvious.

"Yeah, but thanks for asking." Now it's him picking at his beer bottle. "It's not why I came to L.A., but it's made me a good amount of money and there's a future there, so how can I really complain?"

"You could still try to make it as an actor."

He stares over at me, his blue eyes holding just a note of disappointment. "I know."

I let the conversation stall and eventually the two of us rest our heads on the back of the seats. If only I could get rid of this cagey feeling I have just under the surface. Everything is going great. We're on the way to Chicago to meet the investor and check out locations. Layla is done filming, spending time with the kids at home. All the boxes are checked. So why can't I help but feel like it's all about to come crashing down?

———

"Make sure you smile. You've got that resting bitch face thing going on when you aren't smiling." Jagger fixes my perfectly knotted tie—again—and then brushes his hands down my arms.

"I'm not five, asshole. Besides, I don't think resting bitch face is even a thing for men." I push him away from me.

He gives me a quick once-over. "I beg to differ." We both step into the elevator. "You're practically a baby in this industry."

"I was a producer for more than eight years. I know this industry, jackass." The elevator doors open and I file out before him.

His shoes click on the floor beside me as we make our way to the restaurant. His body language screams poise, confidence and privilege and I'm hoping mine does as well. I'm about to throw up, but I'd never tell him.

We walk to the restaurant of the hotel where Hannah wanted to meet us and Jagger takes the lead with the hostess.

A second later, Jagger's gaze is homed in on the ass of the cute hostess while we follow behind. My nerves are shot, my anxiety starting to make sweat form under the collar of my shirt. I plaster on a smile so wide, my cheeks fucking hurt.

*Damn it. Calm down. You got this.*

Her only stipulation was Layla, who we have.

The little devil on my right shoulder reminds me that I only have her until I tell what I did, but I can't pay any attention to that evil voice because the hostess extends her hand. Jagger approaches and there she is.

This woman is a few years older than me. She's dressed in

a revealing red dress that dips down between her breasts. She's definitely someone I can see tests Jagger's 'no sleeping with clients' rule. Technically, she's not a client, but he does have to work with her.

Jagger shakes her hand, kissing her cheek and then stepping aside.

"Hannah Crowley, meet Vance Rose."

Her red-lipsticked mouth smiles, revealing perfectly white teeth. She extends her hand, bracelets adorning her wrists, a simple ring on her right hand.

"Don't you mean Ryder Stone?" She side-eyes Jagger, who chuckles, looking at me.

The reference to my producing alias only brings Layla to mind.

Before I have time to say anything, she shoos me off with her manicured hand. "I'm kidding." I shake her hand. "Very nice to meet you, Vance."

"You as well, Ms. Crowley."

"No, no, no, it's Hannah," she insists.

Jagger steps back and holds her chair out for her. The three of us sit down, Jagger taking the spot in the middle.

"Why do you seem to look younger every time I see you?" She holds her hand out to Jagger and then shakes her head. "The fact men become more handsome with age and woman become hags is total bullshit. Just ask my ex-husband. I'm pretty sure it was the year I turned thirty that he started heading to college campuses for younger versions of yours truly." She laughs, but it's empty and bare.

"I can't imagine that, Hannah." Jagger leans forward, lowering his voice. "You have the best ass in this place." He winks.

She hits him on the shoulder and laughs, then turns her attention to me. "This is why I keep Jagger around. He's good for the ego."

I could add my two cents. She *is* gorgeous. She's turned at least five heads since we've been sitting here. It's more than the red dress, though. It's her demeanour, and her sophistication. The 'take no shit' attitude pours off of her.

"He only speaks the truth," I say.

She sips her wine. "I need to keep both of you around for a while. Going through a divorce when your husband somehow beat you to the best lawyer in town hasn't been good for my self-confidence. Or my bank account." Again, an empty laugh leaves her lips.

The waiter comes over, Jagger and I order drinks and then I wait for her to open her menu before I do.

Between some small talk about what's good at the restaurant and Jagger pouring on enough compliments that she's probably sweeter than a jar of maple syrup, we order and afterward the real conversation begins.

"I have a question, Hannah," I say.

Jagger looks at me with a warning in his eyes.

"Yes?"

"You told Jagger my story reminds you of your own love story..."

She purses her lips as though she's trying not to remember, but eventually her entire face relaxes. "Confusing, right?"

"A tad," I say.

"Well, I wasn't a criminal and neither was he, but when I read your story, I just felt how overpowering to was for Melanie to have Joseph dominate her life. The summer before I went to college, I fell in love with this guy. He was a few years older than me and I would've followed him anywhere to do anything, like Melanie did Joseph. Melanie's love for Joseph reminded me of myself during that time in my life." Her smile dims for a second and she picks up her wine to sip it. She might physically be at the table, but mentally I can tell she's far, far away somewhere in the past.

"Was it Todd?" Jagger asks, and I'm assuming Todd is her ex-husband.

"No. I married Todd because I was an idiot." Her tone brings a finality to the conversation.

"The script manager thinks there isn't enough love in the script." I ask her opinion—if she's bankrolling it she'll tell me the truth.

"There is on Melanie's side for sure," she says.

At least that's one part I don't have to worry about.

"So, you guys have secured Layla Andrews?" she asks, her gaze bouncing from me to Jagger.

"We have," he says. "Why did you want her again?" Jagger discreetly looks at me and I know he's trying to see how invested Hannah is in her. "Do you know her?"

"No." She laughs. "I don't know her, but I watched a film she starred in right after her stint on that kids' channel was over. Anyway, it got me thinking how she's had nothing but secondary character roles as an adult. I think she'll be a good Melanie. She's a fresh face and she's due for her spotlight. Why not utilize someone new and different rather than an overused actress with a bunch of roles behind her? I want people to *see* her as Melanie."

"Those overused actresses put asses in the seats," Jagger says, but smiles. "But fresh faces, as you say, can do it, too. If we're lucky it'll be known as her breakout role a decade from now."

"What film did you see her in?" I ask and Jagger shoots me a glare.

"Um..." Her fingers drum along her lips. "*Polarized.*" She points to me. "It's about a girl who suffers from bipolar disorder in college. Very dramatic and really well done."

Huh, I've never heard of it.

"I'll have to watch it, I'm not sure I remember that one," I say.

"It went straight to DVD." Jagger fills me in.

"You really should watch it," Hannah says to me. "Oh, and who are you thinking for Joseph? Wait!" She sits up straighter, clearly excited for whatever she's going to say. "How about Carver Sterling? They're married, right?"

Jagger's eyes widen and he picks up his drink and takes a large sip.

"Actually, they're getting divorced," I remark.

She slouches down in her chair. "That's too bad, because he might be a good fit. It'll definitely be on everyone's radar if it's the film that put their family back together." She laughs.

Our salads arrive and I unwrap the silverware, placing my napkin in my lap, taking extra care to concentrate on the task before I bend over the table and tell Hannah that Layla's taken, and not by Carver Sterling.

"We can definitely keep that in mind." Jagger takes the lead on responding, which I'm thankful for.

"I'd love to fly out when you start doing casting." She picks up her fork, mixing the lettuce around with her fork. "I want to start filming this summer. I have a few Chicago locations in mind."

"We'll get everything sorted once we finalize all the moving parts of the project." Jagger eats his salad, smiling over a mouthful of lettuce.

"Great. So, are you two ready for me to show you a good time on the town tonight?" Her perfectly arched eyebrows rise and her already huge smile widens further.

"Sorry?" I ask. My plans had consisted of going back upstairs and calling Layla.

"Yes. I need to show you the city where your love story is going to come to life."

I hate that I have to keep an investor happy. My story originated in Climax Cove. Climax Cove and Chicago are drastically different places, but I have no choice. I try reminding myself that it would've been worse if I'd sold the script to a big studio—I would have had zero say in anything if that were the case.

"Sounds great. We have another buddy who flew in with us. He'll meet up with us too, if that's okay?" Jagger asks.

"The more the merrier."

I have a feeling I'm not going to be feeling all that well tomorrow morning.

## 19

## Layla

I've lost all energy to move Payne from my lap. We put Via to sleep and he's been so great with Vance the three weeks I was filming that I rewarded him with a movie night. Now the credits are rolling and he's asleep on my lap.

The time on the cable box glows in the dark room. Eleven at night and no text or contact from Vance since he left for dinner. Chicago is two hours ahead, which means it's one o'clock in the morning.

My insecurities wreak havoc on my mind. He could be writing in his hotel room, but Jagger doesn't seem like the type who would let him hole up in his room. And there's the fact Leo joined them, which really means it's more of a guys' trip. Strip clubs. Lap dances. Visions of tabloid photos of sleazy strippers on Carver's lap slam into the forefront of my mind.

Not Vance, though. No way. Then again, I've only known him a few weeks.

Still, in some ways I feel like I know Vance better than I ever knew Carver. I realize now that Carver showed me what he thought I wanted to see. Vance shows me who he really is.

"Ugh." I turn off the television, pick up Payne, and carry him upstairs.

"Vance?" he mumbles.

"No, sweetie, it's Mommy."

He rolls over and clings to his emoji pillow—the poop one —and I laugh at the memory of his arm getting stuck in the machine.

Vance was a real hero that day.

After getting Payne into bed, I close his door, checking my phone once more.

Nothing.

Uneasiness rolls inside my stomach after Payne asking about Vance. He's attached to him. Hell, I'm attached to him. But I've never had a man stick around before. Even my own father wasn't consistently in my life until I was a steady paycheck for him. Then, all of a sudden, I was pretty damn important.

Vance came into this house like a freight train and all three of us hopped on board, with smiles and open arms. The problem is, maybe the freight train was just passing through.

No, no, no. This man-made love to me like no one before. He caressed my body, kissed me tenderly. I have to stop overthinking. Vance isn't Carver.

Feeling a little better after my mental pep talk, I go to bed hoping to be woken up by Vance.

———

THE NEXT MORNING, I'm folding the blanket we used last night and carrying the popcorn bowl to the sink when my doorbell rings.

I glance at the clock. Seven in the morning. The kids are still sleeping. No way it could be Vance unless he caught a red-eye home.

My stomach unleashes dozens of fluttering butterflies. Maybe he's here to surprise me.

My footsteps move faster and faster the closer I get to the front door and my smile grows wider and wider.

I swing open the door. It's not Vance. Instead it's a small Hispanic lady in a pink uniform and a bucket in her hands.

"Hello?" I ask, wondering who the woman is and why she's here.

"Hello, I am Marisol. Mr. Rose sent me." She points to the name on her pink uniform.

*Clean Queen.*

"Why?" I ask, and, without me asking her in, she steps up onto my stoop.

"To clean." She points to her shirt again. "Please." Her smile is kind.

"Okay." I let her in like a fool. "How do you know Mr. Rose?" I ask after she's already inside with the bucket of cleaning products and probably a camera hidden up her shirt.

She hands me her card and I see 'fully bonded' on it, making some of the anxiety that she could be a member of the paparazzi diminish.

"I clean his condo and his friend Leo's. And I practically raised their other friend, Jagger, when he was a boy." Again, her smile is plastered to her lips. She's one happy lady.

I nod a few times, my eyes instinctively moving to the stairway up to the kids' bedrooms.

When a hand lands on my arm, I look up to see Marisol's soft smile. "No worries, Ms. Andrews. I'm very discreet. Jagger refers me to many of his high-profile clients."

"Thank you. Please let me know if you need anything."

She smiles and walks into the family room.

I stand in the foyer, wondering what the hell to do with myself now.

Then I realize it's seven here, which means it's nine in Chicago, so I pull out my phone.

**Me:** *Thanks for sending Marisol. Not necessary, but thank you.*

No three dots appear and I wonder where the hell Vance has disappeared to. The man who texted me from the minute he got off the plane to the time he went to the restaurant has suddenly gone MIA. I search his Instagram and Snapchat account, but no recent posts. He's not even tagged in a post anywhere by Leo or Jagger.

The rest of the morning, I try to stay out of Marisol's way, even leaving for lunch with the kids, although I worry she'd take pictures of my things or steal something the whole time. But if she's a big part of Jagger's life—assuming that's true—then I'm sure I can trust her.

The long-awaited response come comes through at three in the afternoon.

**Vance:** *Hey. Jagger is forcing me to stay another night. He's calling it bonding time. Grrr. Do you have time to talk?*

I hem and haw, staring at the two kids piling ice cream in their mouth. Well, Payne is. Via is wiping whipped cream all over her tray and once in a while she pushes her fingers into her mouth.

**Me:** *I have the kids with me. I'd stay if I were you. Maybe Jagger is coming out this weekend. ;)*
**Vance:** *And to think it's Leo everyone is expecting to. :P*
**Vance:** *I miss you <3*

If he misses me so bad, then why didn't he call me last night and all day today?

**Me:** *I miss you too. Have fun and I'll see you tomorrow.* ☺
**Vance:** *I'm hoping to get in early tonight. Can I call? (Praying hands emoji) Please. LOL*
**Me:** *You can call me whenever.*

My phone rings and Vance's number shows up on my screen.

"Who is it?" Payne asks, rising up on his knees in the restaurant booth to peek over the table.

"Vance."

"Vance?" Payne screams and then looks at Via. "It's Vance."

Although Vance is her play buddy, whipped cream seems like the winner today because she ignores Payne and looks back down at her sticky hands.

"Not quite what I meant," I answer the phone.

Vance chuckles. "Tell me what you're wearing."

Vance's sleepy voice explains why he's just calling me now and my shoulders relax. I hate that I even doubted him.

I look down at myself. "Jeans and a sweater." I turn my head to the side to muffle my conversation from the kids. "Not an inch of my body is showing."

He groans. "That's all right. I have a good imagination and an even better memory."

"I'm sure." Payne reaches for my phone, but I hold my finger up to him.

"Don't you want to know what I'm wearing?" His tone is filled with mock offence and I can't help the smile that finds its way to my face.

"Payne is about to strip the phone away from me." I giggle the schoolgirl laugh he always seems to pull out of me.

"So we'll table the phone sex for now. Do you think you can get a babysitter for Sunday night?"

My belly tingles with excitement that he's asking for alone time with me.

"I can try. My parents are returning in a few weeks, but I might be able to get my friend's daughter to help out, since it's a weekend." A loud banging echoes out across the line and I pull the phone away from my ear. "What is that?"

"Jagger and Leo. We're heading to a location Hannah wants us to see." More background noises filled with the rustling of sheets and what I think is him walking toward the door.

"Hannah?" I ask, trying to keep my voice even-keeled.

"Hannah Crowley, the investor."

I nod, although he doesn't see it.

"I think she has a slight crush on you." He chuckles.

"I think she wants to grind pussies with you," Jagger yells in the background.

"Too bad. I'm the only one who'll be grinding your pussy," he whispers into the phone and my entire body suddenly feels like it's on high alert.

I cross my legs to try to ease some of the tension brewing. "Well, then you better hurry home. I'm lonely."

"Yeah, me too. I beat off once last night and once this morning thinking of you."

I try to push the image from my mind, but it's near impossible. The thought of him stroking himself while thinking of me is off-the-charts erotic.

I clear my throat. "Good to know. Thanks again for Marisol. She did an excellent job."

"There's my sweet girl." I can hear his smile.

"Okay, love birds, chirp chirp, let's go!" Jagger screams in the background.

"What do you mean?" I ignore the annoying best friend.

"I don't know. You seemed distant until just now. Maybe it's just the miles between us."

I'll keep my insecurities to myself. He doesn't need to know Carver's infidelity has left scars that are still healing. He doesn't need to know that for half the day I imagined him in bed with another woman. Those are my issues, not his. "Yeah, it's weird. You've been a part of our lives for only weeks, yet all three of us seem to feel your absence when you're gone."

He chuckles. "I feel the same. I might be losing at this whole guys' trip. I almost fell asleep at the bar last night."

I bite down my smile. "Well, you go and have fun."

"Me!" Payne reaches again.

"All right, I'll be back in town tomorrow afternoon. Work on that babysitter."

"Wait, Payne wants to talk to you."

"Come on, man, let's go," Jagger says in the background.

"You go and I'll meet you in the lobby," I make out Vance saying, even though he's trying to muffle the phone.

"I'm leaving in five minutes whether you're there or not," Jagger says in his usual bossy manner.

"Bye, Layla," Leo says and then I hear a door shut.

"Finally." Vance comes back on. "Give me Payne."

I hand the phone to Payne, who sits back in the booth with his water in his hand and a big ol' smile on his face. "Hi," he says in an excited voice.

The two talk for a minute about when Vance will be back, what he's doing, and who he is with while I try to clean up Via as best I can. One thing I can admit is that being with the kids by myself again, after not being that way for weeks, has made the lonely hole in my chest a little wider.

"Yeah, here's my mom." Payne holds the phone to me, but then takes it back. "Love you." And then he holds the phone out, but I'm too stunned to actually grab it.

My slow reaction causes him to let it go over the top of his melted ice cream sundae and it splashes onto the table when my phone hits the bottom of the cup.

"No!" I scream, my hands moving for the sticky, dripping wet phone. I wipe it down and press the home button. Nothing.

Dead, and now I have no idea what Vance might be thinking. Great.

"I'm sorry," Payne says with watery eyes, staring at the phone.

I muster up a smile. "That's okay, buddy. It was an accident. Let's go to the phone shop and maybe we'll do a bit more shopping if your sister cooperates."

Mommy needs some retail therapy all of a sudden.

———

By the time we reach the house, my new phone is in my purse, Via is hanging in my arms and I'm clasping a bag of takeout for dinner. Payne runs in first, and I place Via down on the floor for her to run around while I get us situated.

"Payne, turn off the television," I say, hearing the sound of Backyardigans coming from the family room. After the day I've had I cannot stand to listen to those singing and dancing non-animals.

"I didn't turn it on." I catch him in the fridge grabbing a drink.

I freeze as I set the takeout bags on the counter. I deactivated the front door alarm when I walked in, I know I did.

I wave my hand for Payne to come back to me. He does, but in doing that Via has her eyes on what's going on. She runs right into the room.

"Stay here." I place my hand on Payne's chest and run after her.

Seconds before I enter the room I hear her giggling.

I step into the room and see the back of a man bending down to pick up my little girl. I'd know the back of this man anywhere—that short blond hair and those strong shoulders. Carver slowly turns, flashing me what started as his 'get in my pants' smile and over the years of his bad behavior morphed into his 'get out of jail free' smile.

"Layla." His voice is laced with the sweetness he uses when he wants forgiveness.

"Carver," I return, my voice laced with annoyance.

"No welcome home hug?" he asks. Via wraps her two arms around his neck, squeezing him tight.

I stare in disbelief, wondering why the hell he's back, when Payne's hand slowly slides into mine, reminding me that for his and Via's sake, I have to play nice.

**20**

**Vance**

"So, all in all this weekend was pretty kickass." Jagger sits down across from me at the restaurant in the airport. "I think Hannah's smitten with you." He smiles over the rim of his mug.

"She's loving her single life," Leo says while he adds about an inch of jelly to his toast.

"She's only in her thirties and got hosed for all that fucking money in the divorce. I think she's doing what she wants now and it's a smart decision on her part to invest in films." Jagger places his hand on my shoulder. "This guy's film to be specific."

I smile and snap a piece of bacon, popping it in my mouth.

The weekend was a success and I fully believe Hannah will work with me with or without Layla, but obviously she has her heart set on Layla starring in the film.

"Just so you're aware, I'm taking Layla out tonight and confessing my sins." I eye Jagger.

He rolls his eyes and blows out a breath. "I don't understand why you're going through all this for a girl you'll probably be broken up with in a month or two."

"Jag." Leo shakes his head, piling another forkful of eggs into his mouth.

"Leo, you've dated enough actresses to know. There's no settling down long term with them," Jagger says.

Leo shrugs, looks over to me. "Why burst the bubble now? Let them have their fun."

I shoot him a 'what the fuck' look. I thought the guy was on my side?

"He's putting the entire film on the stove with the gas on. One tiny spark and the whole thing combusts."

I stand up, forcefully shoving my chair back from the table and stalking away. I've never seen Jagger be this big a dick before. Correction: I've never seen Jagger be this big a dick *to me* before.

Fifteen minutes later, Jagger sits next to me at the gate. Our plane is here, but we're not allowed to board yet.

"I'm sorry," he says, tapping his legs.

"Just forget it. My business is my business from this point on."

I spy Leo in the gift shop across the way, probably trying to give Jagger and I time to figure this shit out.

"I don't want that. I like picking on you." He nudges me with his shoulder.

"I'm over it, Jag. I'm with Layla and I know you don't agree, but speaking your displeasure at every turn is getting pretty fuckin' old."

He nods slowly a few times. "Yeah, okay. I'll keep my mouth shut. I just want you to seize this opportunity, you know? The script is great. Not to mention, when it comes to you and Leo, I've always considered myself the big brother of the group, watching out for you guys in the cesspool that can be L.A. life." His lips turn down at the corners and I can see that he's sincere.

Jagger was a lifesaver to Leo and me when we first arrived. Everyone knows everyone in this town and things don't work like they do everywhere else in the world. Maybe he's failed to see we've grown up. We're not those wide-eyed guys looking at the hookers and dealers on Sunset anymore. He needs to trust us that we each know what's good for us.

"I like her... a lot." I face him head on so he can see how important this is to me.

It's been a short time, but there's something with Layla that just fits. I can't lie, the fact her son told me he loved me on the phone did knock me off balance a little, but he's four and it's pretty cool to think he likes me enough to say that.

"Okay then. My lips are sealed." He stands up, walking backwards away from me. "I won't even razz you when and if it blows up." He winks with his classic grin and then he joins Leo in the gift shop.

Leo looks back at me, eyebrows raised, silently asking if all is well again. I nod.

All this talk about Layla makes me miss her.

I pull out my phone as the flight attendant tells us that the plane will begin boarding in a few minutes. Since we're first class I know we'll be called soon.


**Me:** *Were you able to get a babysitter for tonight?*
**Layla:** *Looks like it.*
**Me:** *Great, I'll pick you up at seven.*
**Layla:** *Why don't I meet you at your place for a change?*
**Me:** *This is a date. I'll pick you up. ;)*
**Layla:** *Can you talk?*


The hairs on the back of my neck stand on end.

**Me:** *I'm about to board. Something up?*
**Layla:** *No. I just have to tell you something. It can wait until tonight.*
**Me:** *Great. Me, too. See you at seven.*
**Layla:** *I'll wear a dress. ;)*
**Me:** *Easy access. I like how you're thinking. I'll go commando. ;)*
**Layla:** *Be careful with those zippers.*
**Me:** *Don't worry about me, I'm a pro.*

Leo smacks me on the shoulder. "Let's get home." During all the texting I must have missed our announcement to board.

**Me:** *Boarding now. See you tonight. <3*
**Layla:** *Can't wait.*

———

I STEP out of my car and walk up to the front door. By the time I got home, showered, and changed I had no time to relax, but I was able to catch up on sleep on the flight home.

When we separated, Jagger and Leo wished me good luck with telling Layla the truth tonight. I thanked them because I need all the luck I can get. I'm praying tonight ends with my mouth on her pussy, not her foot up my ass.

I wipe my clammy hands down my jeans and ring the doorbell.

Small footsteps sound from the other side and my heart warms knowing that Payne is going to be on the other side of the door to greet me.

"Never answer the door on your own," a male voice says and the footsteps stop.

What the fuck? She hired a guy babysitter? It better be her father or a brother I don't know about.

The door opens and my stomach drops to my feet, nausea sweeping in fast and furious. My worst fear just came true.

"Holy shit. Layla's going out with you?"

"Carver?" My eyes have to be playing tricks on me. Her ex-husband is here and he's answering the door like he fucking lives here?

"I haven't seen you since that guest role on *Abandoned*." He shakes my hand, a little firmer than I remember.

"Yeah," is all I manage given that I'm still in a state of shock.

"Are you guys in production right now?" he asks and my gaze moves to Payne, who is standing in the doorway of the foyer and living room.

"Hey, buddy." I raise my hand for a high-five and Payne comes over and smacks it.

"Yeah, Payne was telling me about how much he likes you. So, did you leave executive producing for nannying?" Carver laughs, ushering me into the house.

He continues to walk into the living room and I follow him since he's yet to stop talking.

"I had no idea you went by a different name." He sits down on the couch, Via nowhere to be found.

"Um..." I glance around, seeing no sign of Layla. "Yeah, I used a different name for all my production credits."

He nods. "You and me both. My real name isn't Carver Sterling."

Go figure. I never even asked Layla if it's her real name. Maybe it's not and she'll understand.

"Hey." He leans in closer. "Does Layla know?"

I avoid his question and respond by saying, "I'm no longer with *Abandoned*."

He chuckles. "No shit." Then he holds his hands up. "I mean, news travels fast over pillow talk."

I nod. Of course, he knows all about why I got fired

when he's been banging the instigator in question. I should have known better than to think Gwen would keep her trap shut.

"But does she know about you being executive producer of *Abandoned?* Does she know you're Ryder Stone?" The smirk playing on his lips can't be mistaken for anything but a power trip over the fact that he has something over me.

"What?" Layla's voice appears behind me. "This is Vance Rose, Carver."

I turn around and all the breath in my lungs rushes out. She's wearing a cute flower dress with a jean jacket and a pair of flats, her legs long and tanned. I hate the fact that Carver is getting to see her looking so amazing, too.

"You sure about that? Guess it's my mistake." Carver laughs and sits down on the couch, grabbing his beer like the lights just flickered and it's time for the show to start.

And from Layla's confused face, I know it's going to be a show.

"Hey, can we talk?" I whisper, reaching out for her hand.

She eyes me suspiciously and then glances at Carver, but her gaze travels back to me.

"You sure you're good with the kids?" she asks him.

Payne is sitting on the couch playing with the iPad.

"Yeah, Olivia's down for the count for the night and me and this guy are gonna watch the fight." Carver uses his foot to get Payne's attention, but Payne never looks up from the iPad.

"Call me if you need me." She moves over to the chair and kisses Payne on the top of the head. "Be good for Daddy, okay?"

Payne nods.

"Nice seeing you again, Carver." I hold my hand out to Carver and he shakes it, his smug look still in place.

"You too, Stone." He winks.

Layla bunches up her forehead and turns to look at her son. "Payne, baby, do me a favor and go upstairs."

Payne ignores her.

"Layla, let's go talk," I say.

She shakes her head. "Payne!" For the first time since I've known her she raises her voice to him.

It works as intended, garnering his attention.

"Upstairs, now." She points to the stairs.

"What did I do?" He looks between his mom and dad, then lastly my way.

"Nothing. I'm sorry for yelling. We just need a little adult time."

Payne stands and she kisses the top of his head again before he runs upstairs with the iPad.

"Layla, let's go." The last thing I want is to have this conversation with her shitty ex taking notes from the sideline.

She stares up toward the stairs. Payne's door shuts and her head slowly swivels toward me, her eyes firing cannonballs in my direction.

"Why is Carver calling you Stone?"

Carver laughs.

"Quit it, Carver." Her head snaps back and forth between the two of us.

"Can we talk about this alone?" I ask.

She crosses her arms, inhales a deep breath, and then storms into the kitchen.

"Good luck, man. There's a reason we're getting divorced," Carver says.

I flip up my middle finger as I walk into the next room.

She's pacing back and forth in front of the kitchen counter when I get there, but her shoes stop clicking on the hardwood floor as soon as I enter.

She stares back at me and dread fills my veins. "Answer the question. What is your real name?"

"My name *is* Vance Rose, but—"

"Tell me, Vance." She crosses her arms and cocks a hip to the side.

"Let me explain from the beginning," I plead.

"Answer the question and I'll decide if you should explain or not."

Her lips are already turned down, her eyes about to throw fire my direction. Which seems fair. I already burnt her in the past, suppose she should do the same. My shoulders sag with remorse, not only for what I did to her in the past, but for hurting her again now.

"I was an executive producer under the name Ryder Stone." My fists are clenched at my sides as I wait for her reaction.

Her arm extends, her finger pointed toward the door. "Get out." Her nostrils are flaring, her arms shaking.

"Let me explain." Panic grips me and makes it hard to breathe because I *cannot* lose this woman. Or her kids. They mean too much to me.

"You walked into this house, into my life. You hugged my kids all while knowing you were lying. You're a bastard, whoever the fuck you are. Now get out of my house and out of my life." She faces the doorway and when I glance behind me, Carver's leaning against the doorframe, his beer at his lips.

There's no way this conversation can happen while that fucker is here.

I stare at her for a minute and she's so disgusted that she can't even keep her gaze on me and she looks away. Pain lances through my chest knowing that I did this to myself. I have no one else to blame. The devastation and self-hatred

I'm feeling make me want to lash out and it's all I can do to keep a hold of myself.

I'm not letting her go without a fight. I refuse.

"When you're ready for me to explain, call me."

I step back and walk through the house and out the door with tears stinging the corner of my eyes. Will this be the last time I set foot in this house? That thought is too painful to bear and has me wiping at my eyes.

I'll give her the space she needs tonight, but I'm not done fighting for us.

## 21

## Layla

T*hump.*

My head hits the kitchen table when the door shuts. He's gone.

"What an asshole." Carver sits down at the table.

I grab his beer and swig down a hefty amount. "And you're not?" I ask, but the question is mumbled into my sleeve.

"I was. Past tense."

I peek my eyes up above my sleeve. He's got to be kidding me. Sitting up straight in my chair, I cross my arms and look him over. He's his usual put-together self with a new haircut and shave. No stains on his clothes or dark circles under his eyes from partying all the time. "Why are you here?"

His face distorts into an expression that flashes hurt for a second and then it's gone. Like always, he diverts his gaze, stands and tosses one beer in the recycling and grabs another one from the fridge.

"Carver." I wait for him to answer.

There was a time he intimidated me. He's a few years older and in my eyes, he knew everything. He'd come up through the same big platform I had and I thought he'd protect me, understand me. Instead, I have two kids and a cheating almost ex-husband. This is not how I imagined my life at twenty-eight.

"Truth?" he says.

"If you think you can tell me without bursting into flames."

His lips turn up. Mine remain straight. His flirtatiousness won't work on me anymore.

"I saw the tabloids." He shrugs.

"You saw what?" The press haven't been able to get a visual of Vance besides the back of his head yet. Hence the reason his lie lasted so long.

"When I saw you were seeing someone... I didn't like it. The fact he turned out to be the guy who got you fired and so you tossed his ass was just a bonus."

I clench my teeth together. This man has some nerve after everything he's put me through. Did he give any thought to how I might feel as his *wife* when he was balls deep in other women? "I'm not going to discuss my personal life with you. Regardless, you're a father of two children—you better start acting like it. Payne feels uncomfortable around you."

"Why? I'm his father."

My hand smacks the table. "Donating sperm doesn't mean that you're forever in his heart. You have to be here, Carver. Spend time with him, kiss his boo-boos, play superheroes with him, plan birthday gifts, take him to the movies, read him books, make him feel like he matters. That's being a father."

I take a deep breath after letting all the frustration that's been welling up inside me for months escape. Carter looks on wide-eyed, knowing better than to try to interject when I'm like this.

"I know this industry makes some things impossible, that

there'll be times you're away filming, but you're not even trying."

He picks at the label of his beer bottle, staring at his handiwork for a moment after removing it without any residue.

"Carver." I sigh.

"I know. I know." He breathes in deeply again, and his eyes finally meet mine. "I know."

"You can't have it both ways." Needing a drink of my own, I grab a wine glass and a bottle from the refrigerator, pouring myself a healthy amount.

Carver comes up behind me, his hands on my waist, his lips on my neck. For a moment I remember how much I once loved him. But now his lips feel cold and his hands make me shrink.

I slip away from him.

"What the fuck?" he says.

His head tilts to the side, a questioning look on his face. He's gorgeous, there's no refuting, but he doesn't have an honest bone in his body. At least when it comes to me. Quite simply, he's not the type of man I need or want in my life.

"I thought maybe with that jackass out of the picture, we could give it another go." He approaches and I step back until the cool metal of the fridge hits my back. "We were good together. Hollywood's number one up-and-coming couple. Fans rooted for us." He cages me in, his arms on either side of my head while he peers down at me. "You haven't forgotten how good we were in bed, have you?" He bends down again, but I crouch under his arm and grab my wine glass from the counter.

"Not happening, Carver. I'm with—"

"No, you're not. That jackass killed your career. Do you not remember how many nights you cried after you were fired from that part? That was going to be a great opportunity for you."

I do remember. It was going to be my first big break as an adult outside of the typecast roles of a pretty, gum-popping teenager from my youth.

"It's none of your business," I snip.

My phone dings on the table and I start walking over to get it, but Carver beats me there and swipes it off the table.

"Give it to me, Carver. What are you, twelve?"

"Jackass says he's sorry and he wants to talk. That guy needs to get a family of his own. No way he's going to sneak in and grab my family out from under me." He drops my phone on the table and I pick it up.

"I hate to break it to you, but you're not a part of this family. You haven't been home in months."

He grabs my free hand. "I'm here now. Let's try this."

"Mommy?"

We both turn to see Payne standing in the doorway. I pull my hand from Carver's.

"Where's Vance?" he asks.

Carver's deep, annoyed breathing sounds from behind me.

"He had to leave."

"I'm here, buddy." Carver comes right next to me, squatting in front of Payne.

Payne's gaze bounces to him and then back to me. "Can I watch television?"

I nod. "Sure."

"Hey, buddy. Do you want to go to the zoo tomorrow?" Carver asks him.

Payne shrugs his shoulders, grabbing a blanket and crawling up on the couch.

"Buddy?" Carver tries again, but he ignores him and heads into the family room.

"Why don't you try calling him Payne?" I down a gulp of wine. "You do know his name still, right?"

Carver shakes his head. "You're a lost cause."

"No, Carver, you are. Get in there and watch television with him. Talk about the show. Talk about his favorite superheroes. Just try to have a relationship with him. If you'd already had a good one then Vance would have never felt like a threat to you." I grab the bottle and my glass and poke my head into the family room. "Sweetie, Mommy is going to go upstairs. Your dad is going to get you ready for bed tonight, okay?"

Payne's eyes widen, but when Carver turns his way, he looks back toward the television.

He needs his dad no matter what he thinks right now.

"Go be a father," I say and leave the room.

After I've changed into something cozy, locked the door, and hunkered down under the covers I let the tears come.

How could Vance have lied to me for so long? Why didn't he tell me who he was? I remember how excited I was to be given a role on one of TV's hit shows. To get a call a couple of days before filming started left me devastated.

I wipe the tears from my face and try to ignore the phone that lies beside me on the bed, but it's like a piece of chocolate cake late at night. It's calling my name. After much debate, I grab it and look at Vance's message.

**Vance:** *I'm sorry, please let me explain.*
**Me:** *Was it your decision to not give me that part?*

The three dots appear.
The three dots disappear.
The three dots appear again.

**Vance:** *Yes, but there's more to it.*

I sit there for a few minutes going back and forth about whether to let him explain himself. Then I realize maybe for me to truly put it behind me, I need to hear him out. I'm over taking whatever shit the man in my life wants to dish out. Besides, I have a few choice words for him, too.

**Me:** *Meet me at Cup of Joe at nine o'clock tomorrow. Half hour. That's it.*
**Vance:** *I'll be there.*

There's no explanation for what happened that will appease me. The only thing I want to know is if he thinks I'm not good enough to be in this film either.

———

CUP OF JOE IS BUSY, thankfully, because then I know I won't make a scene. The problem is there are paparazzi outside, so Vance's identity will be out before lunch. I'll have to count on someone else's fuck-up to let me fade into obscurity and off the front page again.

Vance is already in the corner booth with two coffees in front of him.

"Hey," I say, shrugging out of my coat and sliding in across from him.

Two Splendas sit next to my cup with a spoon.

"Thanks." I tear open the packages and pour them into the cup, stirring with the spoon.

"I'm—"

I place my hand up in the air, shaking my head. "No. I'm sure you're sorry. *Now.*"

"I wanted to tell you." He continues to talk but I feel like I have to say my piece.

"If you'd wanted to tell me you would have."

He sulks back in his booth. "True."

"This isn't about you not hiring me—correction, having me fired—from *Abandoned*. It's that you lied."

"I—"

"Please just let me get all this out. It's hard enough." I look over my shoulder, finding a guy immersed in his computer. "And you didn't think I was good enough."

He shakes his head, but it's the truth.

"You probably thought I was still that teeny-bopper actress who was only good for an audience of eight to thirteen-year-olds. You didn't see any value in my talent then, so how can I trust that you do now?"

He sits up straighter. "I do, Layla. I was wrong. So fucking wrong. I'm ashamed to admit it, but there was this other actress, Gwen... and... I did something I shouldn't have."

I ball my hands into fists. "What exactly do you mean?"

He heaves out a heavy sigh. "Gwen and I were sort of seeing each other at the time and she really wanted the part and I agreed to make it happen for her. I did that by throwing you under the bus. I'm not proud of it."

That part went on to be a recurring role for her and shot her up to Hollywood's A-list.

"Did you even feel bad about it at the time?"

Vance pushes his coffee to the side and stretches his arms out across the table and leans in. "I felt terrible. I swear I did before I even knew you. But if I'm honest, at the time I didn't know your body of work after the kids' channel stuff and I wasn't sure you could pull off the role. Now I know I was wrong."

I scoff. "That's convenient. When did you change your mind?"

"After I met you. After Hannah told me to watch a film you were in. *Polarized*."

I take a sip of my coffee, forcing him to wait for my response. "That movie was horrible."

"The movie may not have been stellar, but you… you were brilliant. I may have misjudged you in the past and let my dick rule my thinking by having you fired, but you are supposed to be in my film. This is the role for you. I hope it's a breakout role, but even if the film goes nowhere, there's no other actress who should have it."

"Because of Hannah, right?"

His shoulders sag and he leans back. He's up against a wall, I know he is, but how can I ever trust him?

"Hannah wanted you originally, that's true. Now I want you just as much."

I slide my coffee to the side. "Vance, I'm sorry, but I can't be with you and for that reason I can't take the role. There are so few people in this town I can trust. I thought you were one of them, but you're obviously not. I have no room in my life for people who aren't one hundred percent behind me. My parents use me for money. Friends have used me for connections. I thought you were someone who was going to stand by my side and fight to protect me. Sure, everyone has their ups and downs, but not once did I think you'd intentionally hurt me. Which is what you did when you kept the truth from me. Do you have any idea how hard it is to break out of the child star pigeonhole once this industry has placed you there? Some days even I question whether I'll ever be able to make it happen for myself. I'm at a crossroads with my career and I need people who will help me push my self-doubt to the side and who will believe in me. I thought you were one of those people, but it turns out you didn't believe in me either."

I suck in a deep breath to try and keep the tears threatening to pour from my eyes in place.

"I do believe in you, Layla. You're more talented than

anyone gives you credit for. I'm sorry I acted like a dick, I really am. You'll be happy to know she's the reason I was fired from *Abandoned*."

I won't lie and say there isn't a little satisfaction in knowing that. My curiosity gets the better of me and I have to ask.

"What happened?"

"In a nutshell, she's a crazy, insecure woman and when she saw a make-up artist flirting with me on set one day she lost it. No matter how many times I told her there was nothing going on, a major fight ensued where I told her exactly what I thought of her petty, childish behavior. She didn't much like that and said it was either her or me. They picked her."

I knew I didn't like Gwen. She sounds like a total bitch. Damned if I'll let him know that though.

"Are you giving Carver another chance?" Vance asks before I can even respond to his story about Gwen. His sweet voice has turned venomous.

"To be a father. That's all."

"Still. You forgive *him*. After everything he put you through."

"He's the father of my kids." I sip the coffee.

"So, you aren't getting back together?"

The cup clanks when I place it on the table. "No."

He nods. "What can I do? Surely there's something I do to can prove to you how sorry I am." He reaches for my hand and for a second, I let him hold it. I allow the warmth of his touch on my skin to electrify my body like a good night kiss.

"Nothing." I slide to escape the booth, my hand falling from his grasp.

"Layla, don't go." He grabs my wrist, but I never turn around.

"Bye, Vance." He releases me and I shuffle through the crowded coffee shop.

Once outside, cameras click and paparazzi block my way to the car I ordered. I knew I had to get out fast and didn't need to be fiddling with my keys.

"Who's the mystery man?" one screams.

"Looks like you broke his heart?" another one asks.

"Is it because Carver's back?" the first one asks.

I slide into the back of the car and the driver closes the door, shutting out all the questions, all the pictures.

I'm not sure if Vance's heart is broken, but mine sure is.

## 22

### Vance

My phone rings with my sister's ring tone for the third time this hour. Since it's clear she's not going to take the hint—how Charlie of her—I answer.

"What?"

"Jeez, who pissed in your Corn Flakes? I've been calling you for days," she says.

"Can't you take a hint when I don't call you back?" I mute the television with the hope she doesn't think I have no life. Even though I don't.

She huffs and I can envision her rolling her eyes in my head. "I've known you your entire life. You know that's not going to work with me. What the hell is going on?"

I sigh. "Actually, you've known me *your* entire life. Let's remember who's older, okay? And nothing, just a bad week."

"Does it have something to do with the mom of the little boy and the shit storm of a baby?" There's sympathy in her voice and if I can confess my failure to anyone, it's to my little sister.

"Ding, ding, ding."

"Since the Seattle Seahawks aren't in the Super Bowl, I figure it's a woman issue."

That gets a small chuckle out of me. "I fucked up."

"I'm not surprised. Your communication skills with the women in your life are horrid. Now tell me exactly what you did and we'll assess the damage."

Twenty minutes later, it's out. What I did before I knew Layla, why I got fired from my job, and everything else up until Layla pushed me out of her life. When I'm done with my confessional, she doesn't speak right away.

"Well, how do I fix this?"

Charlie lets out a long, low whistle. "Boy you really fucked up."

"Not helping, Sis." The despair is clear in my voice. I still can't believe I'm not on the couch with Layla and the two kids crawling around us. "You gotta help me. Feed me the bullshit lines about how the excruciating pain will one day disappear. Damn, Charlie, I feel like I'm missing a limb or some shit. Nothing is right in my life since we broke up. And it's not just Layla. I miss the kids, too."

"She's her, huh? The one?" It's not a question, but a statement. One only someone who knows me as well as my flesh and blood could make without me having to say the words.

"I've never felt this way about someone before, Charlie. No matter what I do, I can't stop thinking about her. I keep replaying all the special moments we had and every time a thousand pound weight presses on my chest with the realization I'll never have them again."

"I don't even know where to begin to fix it. Wait it out and she'll come around. If she loves you like you love her, she'll forgive you."

I throw the pillow across the room. "I wish that was the case, Sis, but I think I fucked this up beyond repair."

"I hate hearing you so hopeless," she says with sadness.

My sister might challenge Jagger as the bigger smartass, but when it comes to those she loves, her heart hurts with theirs.

"I should have listened to myself and never got involved. Relationships suck and this will be my last one."

We chat for a couple more minutes and I tell her I have business to attend to. Not because I do but because the whole saying 'misery loves company' is actually untrue. I want nothing more than to be by myself—as alone as I feel inside.

---

"SEE? He's been like this for days." Leo stands in my condo with Jagger behind him.

"Hey, Coop." I pet Cooper and he crawls up on my couch, finding a spot next to my legs.

I click off the television. They don't need to know I've been exhausting the entirety of the Netflix catalogue this past week.

"What is this?" Jagger picks up the pizza box and cookie bin. "What are you, a chick? Where the hell is the whiskey and the hookers?"

"Not everyone deals with a breakup like you." Leo brings the trashcan over, scooping the debris up and placing it inside.

Jagger sits on the chair across from me. "I've never been broken up with." From the blank look on his face, he's serious.

"Never?" Leo asks, huffing as though he must be joking.

"Nope. Never." He shrugs.

"Lucky." Leo picks up the beer bottles and he disappears into the kitchen.

"She was just a chick. Besides, I have great news." Jagger claps his hands and rubs them together.

I glance over at him, not really caring what his news is.

"Hannah has agreed to do the film without Layla." He's smiling, but all I'm thinking about is how I'd like to order another pizza. Maybe I'll lay off on the Italian sausage this time, since last time it gave me indigestion.

"Oh," I say when it's clear he's waiting for some sort of response from me.

My only hope was that Layla might still do the film. Even if I couldn't be *with* her, I'd get to spend time with her.

"Oh?" Jagger yells, glancing to Leo in the kitchen. "This is great news. You don't need the chick in your life or in the movie."

His smug smile unglues me and I stand up, step over my coffee table and grab him by the lapels.

"Whoa!" Leo runs over, placing a hand on my shoulder. "It's Jagger. You know how he is about anything involving feelings."

"What the fuck? Don't you have a fucking heart?" I yell. "Have you ever loved anyone but yourself?" I let him go, although I'd like to see what he'd look like with a shiner courtesy of my fist right about now. Hell, the bastard would probably just figure out some way to use it to pick up more girls.

Jagger stands and straightens his suit jacket. "Then why are you here?"

I plop back down on the couch. "It's where I live, dumbass."

"You asked me if I've ever loved anyone, but let me ask you a question. What is so important to you you'll fight until death to get it? You sat on a script for eight years without doing anything. I thought you wanted that, but then you jeopardize it by getting involved with the lead actress. I'm not saying I was right about this, by the way. If you love Layla, then why are you sitting here wallowing on your couch instead of figuring out a way to win her back?" Jagger takes a seat again and leans back, his ankle resting on his knee.

"She doesn't want to see me. That was perfectly clear."

"And you're just going to accept that?" Jagger asks.

My gaze veers to the kitchen where I find Leo standing waiting for an answer, too.

"I can't force her."

Jagger laughs. "You really do lack any fight. Do you think I stop making calls after the first person turns me down for something I'm trying to make happen for my client?"

"What the fuck do you want me to do?"

"Don't accept no. Win her over. You wrote a fucking romance in the middle of that script of yours. Use sweet words or beg. Do anything, but at least do something. Doing nothing is still a fucking decision whether you want to admit it or not." Jagger's arms are extended and his face is red, his eyes angry.

"What do you care? You don't even like her," I grumble.

His hands ball into fists. "I'm going to beat the living shit out of him." He's looking at Leo now. A few more beer bottles clink into the bag and then Leo's sitting next to me on the couch.

"When you first came to Los Angeles, I remember thinking to myself, how the hell is this guy going to make it? You were so cocky, so arrogant. I thought this town was going to chew you up and spit you back to your small town in Oregon," Jagger says.

I forgot what I was like when I first came here. Everything was so new, so big, but I remember never showing fear or defeat. Never let them smell your fear.

"I know you came down here to be a screenwriter, but you became an executive producer instead. Do you know how many guys chase dreams like that and end up waiting tables their whole life? You made it in this town."

Leo places three beers on the table, snatching one up for himself.

"So what if they fired you? Who gives a shit? It wasn't on grounds of your job performance. It was political bullshit because you pissed off the lead actress you were banging," Jagger chimes in.

I roll my eyes. "That move has haunted me twice now. You were right, I *am* an idiot."

"This is nothing you can't fix. Get off the couch, take a fucking shower, and win this fight." Leo sips his beer and taps his leg for Cooper to come over to him. The dog leaves my side and sits by his owner.

"Get the girl. Live the American dream. I mean, I don't really understand the whole monogamy thing, but you seem to like her." Jagger looks at me with his usual 'whatever' attitude.

"How do I even get her to give me a chance? It's been a month. You've seen the papers."

I glance at the latest magazine with a picture of Carver and Layla at the zoo with the kids on the front—Via in Layla's arms and Payne on Carver's shoulders. That was a sadomasochistic purchase that led to a carton of ice cream being consumed.

*Shit, I am a chick.*

Jagger scoffs. "They aren't getting back together. That was a drop-off. The paps just didn't show the exchange. You know these guys, they'll spin it however it suits them." Jagger dips his head low and, unlike the magazine, his information is legit. "She *has* been spotted out and about though."

I stand from the couch and nod, my mind racing with thoughts of what I can do to win her back. How can I prove to her she belongs to me?

"Don't think. Just do," Leo urges.

"Shower first though. Help the cause." Jagger stands and pushes me toward the bathroom.

With the first small smattering of hope I've felt in four

weeks, I march off to the shower, determined to figure out how to make Layla see how much she means to me.

———

WHY DOES everything always come together in the shower?

I walk out of the bathroom, a towel around my waist, my two best buddies still drinking beer and watching ESPN.

"Do we have to tell you everything? Get dressed, too." Leo laughs at his own joke.

I disregard him. "Jagger, can you get me on *E* or some other entertainment show to do an interview about the film?"

"Why?" He pulls out his phone, scanning through his connections.

"I have to get her attention and let her know I was sincere when I said I wanted her to do the film, so the film is off until she comes back." I turn around and head to the bedroom.

"What?" Jagger's booming steps follow behind. "That's not what I meant."

I shut the door, but he tries the knob and then knocks.

"Are you insane? You're not supposed to give up on your dreams."

I put on jeans and t-shirt, slip into my shoes. I rub the towel on my hair as I open the door. Jagger's face is pale.

"You can't do this." I've never seen him panicked like this before and he's right, it's a crazy move, but one I need to take.

If I can't convince her to take the starring role in my film, it isn't happening. Finding the right fit with another actress has proven fruitless so what's the difference?

"She's the perfect fit and if I can't have her, then I'll write a new script for a new actress."

Leo's staring blankly at me. "Even I'm not in agreement

here. She's still just a girl, Vance. You can't set your dream aside for her."

"I'm not, because the film would suck if she doesn't do it."

"I'm still in talks with two Academy Award-winning actresses. One is very interested and talked about maybe taking a pay cut to do it." Jagger presses a button on his phone. "Victoria. I need you to call all the late-night shows, see if they have any cancelled spots this week." He's about to hang up and then brings the phone back to his ear. "Thanks."

"No other actresses. Only Layla."

"I think he's in sugar shock or something." Leo touches my forehead. "He's gone from no fight to MacGregor in the time it took to have a shower."

Jagger crosses his arms, his phone resting in his hand, waiting for a return call. "I like it. Ballsy and just what you would have done when you came here ten years ago. Now, if she still doesn't take you back, your ass better write a script fast. There's no room at the stabbin' cabin for a deadbeat without a job." He smiles.

Leo shakes his head. "You don't actually call your place that in front of the women you take home, do you?"

Jagger shrugs. "Depends what they're into."

His phone rings and then he walks down my hallway.

"You love her?" Leo asks, a solemn expression I can't explain on his face.

"I do." God, it feels good to finally admit it out loud. Not as scary as I thought.

He nods once and then stuffs his hands in his pocket. "Then you're doing the right thing. Better to have the entire cake than just a slice, right?"

"Yeah."

Jagger walks back to us. "Victoria is starting the rumor that top actresses have been turned down for the role and the script will not be a film unless Layla Andrews is the lead. You must have a horseshoe up your ass because some animal guy had to cancel tonight, so you've got a spot on *Kimmel*, but you only have"—he checks his watch—"an hour to get there."

"Then let's go." I grab my wallet and keys.

"Don't you want to dress in something more appealing?" Jagger asks and I glance down at my casual attire.

"No. This is what I wear."

He shakes his head, placing his hands on my shoulders and turning back toward my room. "Not when you're trying to win a woman over."

"Are you sure you're not the chick?"

————

I sit in the green room, my palms sweaty, my leg tapping. The news hit *E* and *TMZ* about the other actresses being turned down already. It must be a slow scandal day, because normally that wouldn't make it. Then again, Jagger knows people in high places.

"Vance." A young guy walks in to mic me. "You'll be on in about ten minutes. Sit tight and I'll be back in to get you."

Jagger is pacing the room. Leo is busy at the snack area, eating the entire array of chips and cookies. I have no idea how the guy can eat whatever he wants and maintain the muscles he does.

"Did you write down some notes or anything?" Jagger asks.

"No, I'm going to wing it."

"Good man," Leo mumbles over a mouthful of brownie.

Jagger stops pacing. "Wing it? On national television when people are going to wonder why the hell you're even on anyway?"

"Speak from the heart. You know, that beating organ in your chest that keeps you alive?"

"Yes, I'm familiar with it. But that's exactly what it is—an organ. It can't be broken or shattered, nor can it swell when you're in love. If it swells, it means you have pericarditis."

"Peri-what?" Leo asks.

Jagger shrugs. "I fucked an ER doctor a few times."

"Ah," Leo and I both say in unison.

"You're crazy." I stand up, thankful to have a friend who makes me laugh right before I'm about to do something that will either make me a complete idiot or a complete genius.

The guy comes back in. "We're ready for you, Vance."

"Great." I walk toward the door.

Leo gives me a pat on the back when I pass him. "Good luck, man. We'll be waiting for you when you're finished."

I turn around toward Jagger. "I hope one day you're lucky enough to get to know what love feels like."

I laugh harder, Leo joining in, but Jagger's face is stone-cold serious.

A woman has to come along one day and make him fall to his knees. A woman other than his long-time housekeeper and nanny, Marisol, that is, because she's the only woman he'd do anything for.

Backstage is a busy place, so I try to stay out of the way as much as possible until I hear my cue to head out there.

"Now, we have a last-minute guest who apparently has something he wants to say to an actress we love, Layla Andrews. Please welcome scriptwriter Vance Rose."

My face heats, my hands sweat, but I walk out to the stage unsure what will happen. This will either be the biggest public flop anyone's ever seen in a long time, or it'll be genius.

Fingers crossed it's the latter.

**23**

## Layla

The doorbell rings and Payne runs to the door.

"Not until I'm here, remember?" I open the door to a smiling Carver.

"Daddy!" Payne runs into the arms of his dad.

In the last month, Carver has impressed me by using all his free time outside of filming to spend time with Payne and Via. I'm not even sure what made him realize he needed to step it up, but this is their first weekend away. The first time they'll be out of my sight with their dad overnight. Carver has spent the night here a few times—in the guest room—but I'm still there.

Carver picks up Payne in his arms. "Hey, Payne."

"What are the beads for?" Payne asks.

I almost choke on my own saliva. How he can remember to ask his dad the question he had last night I have no clue. Kids are priceless.

"Beads?" A deep groove forms between Carver's brows.

"Why are they there?"

"Why are what where?" Carver asks, still not following. And why would he?

Payne reaches down between his legs. "Here."

"Whoa. Okay, don't touch them." Carver shares a look with me that says, *What the fuck is this about?*

"Why don't you talk about it tonight?" I'm barely holding my laugh inside.

Payne squirms and Carver places him down. "Go get your bag."

"Okay." Payne runs out of the room. "I'll grab Via, too."

"Isn't this something we should be talking about together?"

"I don't have beads." I smile.

He rolls his eyes.

I slap him on the shoulder. "This is a daddy job."

"Ha ha."

Payne runs in with his bag, but before he can escape out the door, I grab his arm.

"Hug." I hold my arms out. "I'm going to miss you." I inhale a whiff of his hair and kiss him all over his face. "I love you."

"Okay, Mom." He wiggles out of my hold, wiping his face.

Via walks in dragging the stuffed elephant she loves so much.

"Does she have to bring that thing?" Carver whines like he's Payne's twin.

"She loves it." I scoop her up in my arms.

"Jackass won it for her."

"Who's Jackass?" Payne asks. "Vance won it for her." Then he stares at me. "You said we'd see him soon." His hands land on his hips.

"You did?" Carver asks.

I sigh. "He won't stop asking."

"Rip off the Band-Aid," Carver says, holding his arms out to Via. She leans into his arms with one hand on her elephant, her thumb in her mouth.

"Don't drive fast. Don't hire a nanny. No extra guests." I eye Carver hard on the last one. "Make sure you always have your eye on Via."

"I'm their father, not a stranger." He looks between the kids. "Say goodbye to Mommy."

"Bye, Mommy," Payne says.

Via waves.

I can't believe this is really happening. He's taking them for an entire weekend, leaving me all by myself. What will I do with myself? It feels like a blessing and a curse.

"Watch for the paps," I call out as they head down the walkway. "They've been stuck to me like glue lately."

He waves his hand in the air with Payne's pillow. "I am an actor, too, you know."

I nod, waiting for him to get them strapped in his SUV.

"Don't worry. They'll be back alive on Sunday." Carver drives off and the pit of my stomach hollows.

It's times like this that I miss Vance the most. In the short time we were together he became such a solid foundation to lean on.

What the hell am I thinking?

*No. You hate Vance.*

But even I can't make myself believe it anymore.

———

I'm three episodes in on the first season of *Outlander* when my phone rings.

So annoying. I'm pretty sure Jamie is going to take his shirt off soon.

I slide over the bar without averting my eyes from the TV screen. "You have a question already?" I ask, assuming it's Carver.

"Is this Layla Andrews?" a woman asks.

I pull the phone away from my ear. Hmm. A number I don't recognize. "This is she." My tone is bitter, because after all the precautions I take a damn pap got my number.

"Oh, good. This is Hannah Crowley. I'm not sure you know who I am."

"You're the woman investing in Vance's script."

*Why is this woman calling me?*

"Yes. So, he has talked to you about me?"

"Not really. Just the fact that you wanted me to be the lead. I'm sure you already know by now that it's not going to happen." I lean forward and grab the wine bottle off the coffee table and pour myself another glass of wine.

"I have been made aware of that."

"So, may I ask why you're calling?" I sip my wine, placing the blanket across my legs.

"I wanted you to know that I've given him the investment without you as the actress."

Does she think I'm going to be upset?

"Congratulations." I can't keep the sarcasm from my voice.

"There's a problem. I've just been notified that he won't do it without you."

"What?" My wine glass slips a bit in my hold, but I secure it again.

"You heard me. He doesn't care about my money, if you're not the actress he won't be selling the script and it's such a great script. You've read it, I assume?"

"You assume right. I agree, it's a great script. But Vance and I have had our differences."

She laughs. "A lovers' quarrel, right?"

"Well... yes."

I don't really want this lady in my business. I should be no concern to her, but she really wanted me to have that part and who is to say she wouldn't do the same for another script down the road?

"I got a divorce last year," she says.

Great. This woman thinks I'm Dear Abby.

"Don't worry, this story won't be long. He was a cheating bastard and then he and his prick of a lawyer tried to bankrupt me. Total asshole. Men make stupid decisions. They think with their dick the majority of the time and they think they're always right. They want to be the boss. Am I right?"

I laugh. "You are."

"But one thing that men never do is give up money or a chance to propel their career into the stratosphere for love. It's in their genes, what they're born to do. Be the breadwinner, make the most money. So, the fact that Vance is on national television telling everyone how much he loves you and that he won't make the movie unless you agree to take the role should make it clear how much he loves you."

"Excuse me, what? He's where?" I fumble to find the remote. Damn, it's in the blanket.

"Layla, I told Vance I love your work and you're perfect for this part. At the dinner, he couldn't stop praising you. Give the guy a second chance. Turn the channel to *Late Night*."

*Click*. The line goes dead.

A second later I manage to locate the remote in the blanket and switch the channel and there's Vance.

My heart skips a beat, and I suddenly feel a little dizzy. "Holy shit."

"Many of you don't know me. My name is Vance Rose. I was the executive producer for *Abandoned* for eight years. They fired me last year."

The crowd boos and even Kimmel puts his thumbs down.

Vance chuckles a bit and holds his hand up like it's okay. "They had good reason to fire me. I obviously couldn't spot talent. Long story short, I screwed Layla Andrews out of a part."

The crowd boos again.

"Okay, maybe I have to agree with your employer," Kimmel says and the crowd's boos morph into laughs.

"Yeah, yeah, yeah. Big mistake. That's not even the cherry on top of the disaster I created with her. We made a deal. She needed a nanny and I needed a lead actress for the script I wrote. I didn't think she needed to know my true identity, so I omitted information."

"You mean lied?" Kimmel says and the drums from the house band hit like the punch line of a joke. Vance looks back over at him. "Just trying to keep people interested, man." He laughs.

Vance turns back to look at the television. "Somewhere in the middle of caring for her son and daughter, I fell in love with her. Not her looks, I always knew she was beautiful. I became head over heels in love with her from watching her with her children. The way she juggles the impossible job of fame and motherhood. Her quirky side that makes me laugh. Children, plug your ears."

"This is a PG show, Mr. Rose," the host interjects.

"She's sexy as hell. From earlier than I'd care to admit, she took a chunk out of me. Layla, I really hope you're watching. I'm not doing the film without you. Even if you don't want anything to do with me, take the part. I wrote it for you without realizing. I'm ashamed of what I did, but please know I'm not doing this because I love you and want you back. Well, I do want that. I'm doing this because you're Melanie." Vance turns to Kimmel. "Thanks for having me."

Then like the true introvert he is, he walks off the stage.

*Ring.*

I jolt and grab my phone, looking at the caller ID screen, but it's not the man I want it to be.

Jagger.

"Hey, gorgeous."

"I hadn't even said hello yet."

"I can hear the tears. Why don't you go open your door?"

I drop the phone and run. Then the reality of what is happening slows my pace. I stop in front of the hallway mirror. I look like the working mom of two who thought she'd be staying in alone nursing a broken heart that I am.

I thread my fingers through my hair, pucker my cheeks, and with one last kiss in the mirror, I head toward the door.

Vance is there with a basket full of junk food—pretzels, chips, liquorice and chocolate. Lying right in the middle of the basket is the script.

"Please reconsider taking the role," he says.

"Yes." I nod my head in case my verbal agreement isn't enough.

"Yes?" he questions, a slow smile tugging at the corner of his lips.

"Yes."

"As in a thumbs-up emoji?" He places the basket down on the stoop.

"As in a smiling face with heart eyes emoji."

His head slowly rises. "Are we talking about the part or us?" His voice is soft like a whisper.

"I thought you were asking for forgiveness?" Heat whips up my neck, right into my face.

"I am. But I didn't want to assume. God, are you telling me I can put my arms around you right now?" He reaches out but then he shoves his hands in his pockets.

"They should make a combo hugging and kissing face with closed eyes emoji." I smile and he approaches me.

"Sounds like I need to upload the adult emojis onto your phone." His palms land on each side of my face and he brings his body up flush against mine.

"There's such a thing?" I ask.

"We'll talk about it later." He bends down.

"After what?"

He inhales a deep breath. "After I show you in great detail all the meanings of the adult emojis."

He walks me back into the house and his lips capture mine as the door slams shut behind us. Having his lips on mine again feels so right, as if he's giving me back the oxygen I need to breath properly.

He pulls away and a small sound of displeasure escapes me. I don't want to lose this feeling.

"I love you, Layla, and I'm sorry I screwed up, but what you need to believe is that I'm ready to learn from my mistakes. No more lies by omission. You have my word. I won't do anything to hurt you or the kids. I'm done hurting the people I love. I won't survive losing you all again."

My eyes started watering when he first said he loved me, but the mention of my kids in his declaration of love has the tears rolling down my cheeks. He uses his thumbs to wipe them away.

"I love you, too, Vance. I've been so unhappy without you."

"Aw, babe, don't cry." He looks behind him into the house and then swings his head back in my direction. "Where are the kids?" he asks. "I want to apologize to them, too."

"They're away for the weekend with Carver."

Something close to relief passes through his gaze. "I'm excited to see them again, but I'd be lying if I didn't say how fucking happy I am for us to have some adult time together."

I chuckle. "Oh, and what exactly did you have in mind?"

He tilts his head as if he's thinking really hard. "I've heard that make-up sex is the best kind of sex... should we find out?"

I smirk. "We most definitely should."

Before I even know what's happening he's lifted me off the ground and I'm hanging over his shoulder.

"Oh, my God, Vance, put me down."

He only laughs, turning to head into the house and smacking me on the ass as he makes his way toward the stairs.

Call it intuition, call it hope, but something inside me knows that Vance will continue to carry me through life and never let me down again.

---

# EPILOGUE

---

## Vance

### One Year Later

"I REALLY NEED to go back out. Jack is gonna to be knocking on this door again," Layla says. Her hands contradict her words when they descend down to my ass, thrusting me inside of her.

"Jack will wait. I think he's used to your trailer rocking."

Layla smacks me. "Funny, but I don't want him to think I'm some prima donna." Her head falls back. "Oh. My. God. Yes! Right there." A groan escapes her throat.

"So stop, then?" I stop grinding and grin down at her.

Her hand slides to the back of my neck and she pulls me down. I should make her beg, but she's way too tempting for my self-discipline to win this one.

"If you stop I'll kill you."

I chuckle. My hips grind my cock deep and my tongue slides into her waiting mouth.

She lets out a soft moan. "Harder," she says, panting for breath.

I thrust hard into her. "God, you feel so fucking good."

Our quickie in the trailer turns a little more sensual than normal. Half the time, I'm lifting her dress and bending her over the table. You'd think after the year we've been together that we could keep our hands off one another for a whole day.

Nope. We're more on fire for each other than ever.

"That's it. I'm coming," she says and her entire body stiffens right before she falls into the couch, heaving for breath.

I grind into her a few more times, not wanting to come because I could stay inside of her for the rest of the day and still not have had my fill. She lifts her legs and my dick slides deeper, punching up my orgasm like the needle on an engine. I'm in the overheating zone, so I still inside of her, swallowing my own groans and pushing my face into Layla's neck.

I lift my head and kiss her once more before pulling out.

"No sugaring the cookie today?" she asks, sitting up and buttoning up her blouse.

"I figured less clean-up."

She stands and shakes her head. "Not for me," she deadpans.

I snatch her by the waist and pull her down to my lap. "I'll clean you up."

She kisses my cheek and escapes my hold. "Next time I'm holding you to that." She disappears into the bathroom and I finish dressing.

"Hey," I yell to her. "Only two days before the weekend." I do a little dance that she can't see.

"You're that excited to go to Disneyland?" She comes out of the bathroom with her hair styled into a slicked-back ponytail, her dress arranged perfectly on her body and looking like we didn't just fuck.

"I'm excited for the kids this weekend." I pull her into my arms. Payne and Via have been gone for a week with Carver.

"Speaking of..." She widens her eyes. "You can kiss these sneak-aways goodbye for a while once they return."

"There's closets and I can find a nook or two for us to get it on." I raise my eyebrows a few times.

A loud bang hits the trailer door.

"Mommy!" Payne says.

I let Layla go and sneak away into the bathroom. I hear her open the door and the nanny she and Carver share is here for the exchange.

"Thank you. No, we've got it from here. Go take some time for yourself this afternoon," she says. Layla chats up the nanny for a bit about how the trip was.

Payne's footsteps echo in the small trailer as he runs up and down its length. "Vance!"

"Van?" Via says and my heart warms knowing they're looking for me.

Thankfully, that green monster that arose inside me when Carver came back in the picture has been replaced with gratitude at seeing them so happy with both of their parents in their lives.

I open the bathroom door and grab Via as she runs by. She screams and I tickle her chest, making her laugh.

"Vance!" Payne jumps on my back and soon both kids are attached to me.

The trailer door shuts and Layla plucks Via from my arms.

"I missed you," she says, drowning her with kisses. Via swats at her mom, but from the giggles escaping her I know she's loving it.

"What are we gonna do?" Payne asks.

"Well, we have an afternoon of shooting and then we're going to have some fun."

"Yay!" Payne screams.

These kids have it made. Come home from a vacation on an island and then Disneyland that next weekend.

The four of us leave the trailer and head to the studio for filming. We drop off Via at the daycare area we put in for all the employees. That move earned me an extra blow job or two.

I slide up on the chair with my name on the back and Payne hops onto the one with his.

"No nanny today?" Payne asks.

I ruffle his hair. "Who's your manny?" I smile.

"You are!"

"Hey, come here." I motion with my finger for him to come closer.

His smile widens like I just offered him a giant ice cream sundae and he jumps down off his chair and into my lap. "What?"

"What would you think if I was your stepdaddy?"

His eyes bulge out like I just placed the ice cream sundae in front of him with a king-size candy bar sticking out of it.

"You can't tell Mommy." I glance around the studio to make sure she's still in makeup.

"Why not?" He bites his little lip.

"This is going to be our secret until I ask her tomorrow."

He nods his head enthusiastically, the smile never leaving his face.

"So, it's okay with you? You'd like me as a stepdaddy?"

His arms wrap around my neck, but he never answers. I think from the tight hold on me, he's more than okay with me asking his mom to marry me.

"Remember, we have to keep it quiet. Mommy can't know."

Pulling back from me, he nods without saying anything.

"Man, I'm glad that's over. I've been worried all week

about asking you." I wipe the imaginary sweat off my fore-head and he giggles. "You think I need to ask Via, too?"

He shakes his head, scrunching his lips like a grown man stuck in a little boy's body. "Nope. She does what I say, so she'd say yes."

"Okay, everyone," Jack, the director announces as Layla walks out to the set.

Her eyes search us out and she grins.

Man, I can't wait to see the look on her face tomorrow.

———

THE NEXT MORNING, the Andrews household is in complete disarray. I should totally propose on any other day but today. It's clear Carver didn't keep the kids on their regular routine and we're having trouble reining them in. Regardless, I'm happy for them that he's in their lives. At least he's making an effort.

"I think we should scrap Disneyland." Layla might think her voice is low enough, but Payne's head snaps in her direction from where he's getting dressed.

"No," he whines, but even Payne's fight is of dismal proportions.

The kids are tired and Layla and I are exhausted from the shooting schedule.

"Come on, let's go to Yolk Me first and then we'll see how everyone is." I finish changing Via's diaper on the floor of Payne's bedroom, get her dressed and the second I let her go she runs over and hops up on Payne's bed.

"I don't want to make breakfast, but if we go to Yolk Me we'll get there later. Then there will be more people there and it's more likely they'll watch us and take pictures. It'll be a whole fiasco."

I see who Payne inherited his whining abilities from.

"Come on." My heart races. I need to get the question out to her before I die of insomnia. I didn't sleep a wink last night because I was so nervous for today.

Payne stands, but wobbles a little. They're all exhausted. So am I.

"Fine. Let me get dressed quick." She heads to her room and I look to Payne.

"Now's the time, you ready? Remember, don't say anything."

Via slides down off the bed and comes to stand between us, looking between each of us.

"Mum's the word." Payne sucks in his lips.

"Mum?" Via asks.

"Yeah." I laugh at her and she does the same act as Payne with sucking her lips into her mouth.

A half hour later, we walk into Yolk Me, which is way more crowded than we're used to, but it's Saturday. My eyes shoot to the machine and my heart relaxes seeing the out-of-order note taped to the glass case.

The owner, who I talked to last week and then again last night, walks up to the hostess station. Unlike the other patrons waiting, Layla seems oblivious that there's a table ready for us. The exact table we sat at the first time we were here together.

"Thank you." I slide in the booth and Payne hops up on his knees right next to me.

"Can I play?" he asks, his eyes shooting from his mom to me. He's brimming with excitement and I can tell that my plan is in jeopardy of being blown if it doesn't happen soon.

"Your mood sure changed," Layla says, digging into her purse for change.

"I got it." I hand Payne a five-dollar bill.

"Me!" Via shouts.

"You're too little," Payne says and then runs over to the game.

Payne inserts the money. Good boy.

"It's out of order," Layla calls over, but Payne moves the crane.

"Guess not," I say and Layla shrugs, looking over the menu.

She's so calm, I'm certain she has no idea what's about to happen.

"Me!" Via says again.

Layla's hand instinctively moves to her daughter's arm, her eyes not even coming off the menu. But Via is having none of it.

"Me play!" Via is on the verge of a scream.

"Let's just order." Layla dips her menu down, her gaze finding mine with a look that says, *This was a bad idea, we should all be at home.*

"It's fine." I smile.

Our waitress comes over and Layla orders for her and the kids. Then I order for myself. The entire time, we've both tried to calm Via down, but she keeps trying to free her legs from her high chair. I think she might be trying to bungee-jump from the thing.

"Come on." I stand up, and unbuckle her.

"She won't get back in now." Layla shakes her head like Via will be my problem, stirring her Splendas into her coffee.

Via tries to use the crane one time and Payne tries, but neither can get it, which is good.

"Go ask your mom to come over," I whisper to Payne and he nods enthusiastically, running over to his mom.

Layla's attention is stuck on her phone.

"Mom!" Payne yells and she startles, her hand gripping her heart.

"You scared me." She laughs and her eyes find me and Via over at the machine.

"Will you help me?" Payne asks, portraying his best 'please, Mommy' face.

"Vance is there. Can he not get it?" She's already sliding out of the booth.

I knew she couldn't resist the urge to beat me at something. If she thinks I couldn't get the animal and she can, she'd jump at the chance.

"No, I need your help, Mommy." Payne waits outside of the booth while Layla gets up and heads over to the machine.

"You couldn't do it, huh?" she asks in a cocky voice.

I shake my head. "Don't be too sure until you get the animal yourself."

She shrugs one shoulder. "I'll get it." She weaves her fingers together, stretching them to crack her knuckles. "Want to see the master?" she asks Payne, who's jumping up and down.

If she doesn't get the loosely placed blowing-kiss-faced emoji pillow I'll be the one reaching my hand up there like Payne did.

"You want the angry face one?" She looks down at Payne.

"No!" he yells, his face transforming into an 'are you stupid' expression.

"Hey, that's not the way you talk to me." Layla's attention shifts from the game to correcting Payne's behavior.

We really don't need a detour into parenting our child right now.

"Sorry." Payne's head dips down.

"Let's win one for Via," Layla says, searching the game.

"The blowing kiss one," I suggest and she looks over her shoulder at me.

"One of my faves." Then her attention goes back to the game.

I nudge Payne's shoulder, having him come over to my side, trying to get the sour look off his face. This is a happy time.

"I'm not sure I can get that one. I think I should go for the heart eyes one." Layla's speaking while all her focus is on the pillows.

*Oh, hell, no.*

"Just try. You get to keep going until you win."

Layla switches gears and moves the crane back, nodding her head in agreement. She presses the button and the crane lowers. My girl is good. First try and the pillow is up in the claw.

"Oh, yeah." Layla does a running man and the three of us laugh. "I got it. Who is the master of this game?" She turns around, tickling Via.

"Cool your jets, Vanilla Ice."

She laughs at me, grabbing the pillow from the slot and handing it over to Via.

"Don't you think you should look it over before giving it to her?"

Her face crinkles, but she looks it over anyway. Her palm must land on the pocket I had sewn in.

Payne's eyes light up as he stares up at her. I place Via down on the ground, linking her hand in Payne's. Payne grips it tight like I told him to do.

"What is th—" She pulls out the ring and her face reddens. "Vance?"

I grab her hands, kneeling on the ground in front of her. I take her hand in mine.

"Layla, I knew after three weeks that I wanted to marry you, and I've sat back, waiting for all the pieces to fall into place." I glance to the kids and then back to her. "I know you just got your maiden name back legally, but I'm asking you to change it again."

She laughs. Her divorce was only final six months ago.

"To me, you're my sprinkles on a sundae. You're my frosting on a brownie. You're my Splenda in my coffee. You're my sugar on a cookie."

She covers her mouth from laughing.

"You make everything better for me. I was cruising through life doing well, thought I was happy, but I wasn't. After I met you, I realized how much sweeter life can be. Marry me?"

She squats down, holding her arm out so Payne and Via move closer.

"What do you say, guys? Should we marry him?" A tear slips from her eye.

Payne nods and Via tries to grab for the ring.

"Then it's a yes," she says.

Her eyes meet mine and for the first time in my life, my heart pitter-patters.

I place the ring on her finger.

"Close your eyes and cover Via's," I direct Payne and place a hand on each of Layla's cheeks, pulling her down for a kiss.

A few morsels of Splenda sweeten my mouth and I kiss my fiancée, knowing life is only going to get sweeter from here because I have the real thing in my arms, not a fake, artificial substitute. Life is good.

**The End**

The Manny was Piper's idea. She bought a premade cover with a man in an apron under her other author name. Like a lot of premade covers Piper buys, it sat on her computer. She tends to be a tad impulsive when pre-made covers pop up on her feed. Hey, all of us authors do it though.

One day, Piper said "Hey, Rayne, I have this cover" ... and the story idea was ignited. Then came Doggie Style and Chore Play and voila we had the Dirty Truth Series. We were so excited about this series, Piper started writing Doggie Style before we even started the Single Dads Club series.

Then Vance, Charlie's brother came into the picture. We wanted a brother's best friend troupe with Sexy Beast and who else could be the brother but someone from our upcoming Dirty Truth Series? We like to believe in the six degrees of separation with our characters. After Vance was born, we had to decide what kind of guy he was. Although Doggie Style was originally going to be book one in the series, we didn't see Vance as a dog clothing designer. We had to do some rearranging and so we pushed Doggie Style to be book two in the Dirty Truth series.

Vance, The Manny was brought to life and we knew where we had to go after the Single Dads Club Series, but we were in the middle of summer. Kids home from school, which meant Rayne was knee deep in the latest slime recipes, and not getting words in. And seriously, can this slime fad with the kids just die already!?

End of August, our kids went back to school and we worked our fingers to the bone to get The Manny done and complete. We were on to writing Doggie Style when our proofreader told us, you need more scenes. "I need more Manny and not so much Vance and Layla," she said. So, the infamous diaper scene, the ice cream scene and the call from Charlie at the end were last minute additions. What would we do without her? From the early reviews it seems the diaper scene was a hit!

WE'D LIKE to thank our team as always without them The Manny wouldn't be what it is.

- Letitia from RBA Designs for the hot covers and for changing pictures and themes midway.
- RJ Locksley for line editing. Thanks for working just as fast as us to get The Manny back in our hands quick.
- Shawna from Behind the Writer for her eagle eye proofreading skills and her honesty in telling us when we're missing key elements to our story.
- Enticing Journey Book Promotions for their organization and patience. We have to be your

worst clients as far as time line. We promise we'll try harder

- All the bloggers who carved out time to promote us and/or read and review the book.
- Michelle New for yet another set of awesome graphics.
- Our first readers of a really shitty, unedited copy—Heather and Angela.
- All our early ARC readers, first for wanting to read our stuff early and then for posting their reviews.
- And of course, all our unicorns. We made you wait for two months without a book and you're loyalty amazes us. All the unicorn shares, the posts about how much you love our characters. You keep us trucking on this venture. Thank you!
- To all our readers – Thank you for trusting your quality reading time to us. We know there are a lot of choices out there, so we hope you got what we promise to deliver ... humor, heart, heat.

BE on the lookout for Leo in Doggie Style coming this November.

xo,

Piper & Rayne

# ABOUT THE AUTHOR

Piper Rayne, or Piper and Rayne, whichever you prefer because we're not one author, we're two. Yep, you get two USA Today Bestselling authors for the price of one. Our goal is to bring you romance stories that have "Heartwarming Humor With a Side of Sizzle" (okay...you caught us, that's our tagline). A little about us... We both have kindle's full of one-clickable books. We're both married to husbands who drive us to drink. We're both chauffeurs to our kids. Most of all, we love hot heroes and quirky heroines that make us laugh, and we hope you do, too.

Most of all, we love hot heroes and quirky heroines that make us laugh, and we hope you do, too.

*www.piperrayne.com*
authorpiperrayne@gmail.com

## The Modern Love World

Charmed by the Bartender

Hooked by the Boxer

Mad about the Banker

## The Single Dad's Club

Real Deal

Dirty Talker

Sexy Beast

## Hollywood Hearts

Mister Mom

Animal Attraction

Domestic Bliss

## Bedroom Games

Cold as Ice

On Thin Ice

Break the Ice

## Charity Case

Manic Monday

Afternoon Delight

Happy Hour

## Blue Collar Brothers

Flirting with Fire

Crushing on the Cop

Engaged to the EMT

9 798888 714119 0